BLOODLUST

By

KEVAN WORKS

(a love story)

1

She pushed a small table aside, knelt, and picked up a soiled rag from a shallow hole. Placing it on the floor, she pulled the hood from over her head that was worn as a caplet vest revealing long curlicue hair and high cheek bones. The lips were soft red and meticulously painted. The skin was creamy with a delicate manipulation of makeup that was   almost   nonexistent.

She breathed heavily then closed her eyes. For a brief moment, her breathing stopped and she appeared nervous and began to strum her fingers in that, irritating declining mental strain of retardation that forms strange acronyms. Her eyes opened and she reached for the soiled rag and unfolded it. The serpents tongue was exposed to the clammy air and sizzled like water to hot iron. She clasped her hands greedily, touching the top part of her lips with her tongue, breathing through her nose in short gasping spurts. She crossed her arms touching both shoulders, raised her head and chanted the word: **'BENEDICITE'**.

A mysterious wind picked up brushing her hair messily over her face. The piece of flesh began to wiggle and squirm. Her eyes widened behind strong, lengthy, black curls. She sensed what was about to happen and wanted to see. She parted the hair from her face and watched the flesh take shape. It stood erect, then folded. It stretched until it towered over her. It turned within its self.

Nightmarish screams and deceiving whispers floated around her head like a child's imaginary callings from a dark closet. Arms appeared, thick and muscular. Shoulders, broad; were gleaming. The face began to form. Horns tore from the top of its head. Fangs, long and sharp curved under its chin. Pus and mucus poured from its nose. Its eyes opened. Corneas so yellow they were almost caramel in color. It took the shape of neither man or beast, but noticeably praised her lady. Her hands fell dramatically from her shoulders to the floor beside her. The figure was tall, bare to the waist, and from there bristle like hairs reached down like a porcupines back. Its crimped flesh sweated a foul odor that she took in deeply. She raised her hand to her midriff and rubbed smooth to the base of her crotch.

The beast reached out to her and smiled. It stroked her hair and pinched the strands between its twisted fingers. It growled, eyes burning with greed and selfishness bent savagely over her as if to enact a kiss. Its jaws opened revealing smoked skulls for teeth, cracked, and hollowed.

Heavy drops of green waste spilled from the corners of its mouth. She smiled slightly as the toxin burnt through the hardwood floor around her.

It stood erect, letting her hair go with a jerk. It looked around as if the perimeter had been compromised like a soldier who had seen too many battles. It took on the natural stare of its genetics and spoke through a grotesque grin. "The witching hour is near."

2

Amelia, still captivated by the serpents tongue, walked through their spacious twenty-five-thousand square-foot cathedral penthouse to awaken her mate.

They owned the entire building, gutting the top three floors to allow for high ceilings and large antique sculptures. They occasionally entertained guest, which wasn't very often, in the large, roomy airtight apartments on the floor beneath them. They had plenty to choose from because they never rented out the sixty-eighth floor to anyone. The rest of the apartments were packed to the gills with preppies, grads, and lawyers.

There were no walls, as Amelia glided with the grace of a waltz past objects and around eighteenth century furniture. She came upon her lover's bed. He was still as if put there after death. He was pale, shallow, and lifeless. Distinguishing curves surrounded his mouth and brow. His Bavarian silk tux, matted to a desired press accented the blue-blood bow tie under his bulging Adams apple.

The thought made Amelia pull in an even breath. Placing her long painted finger on the creases of his jacket, she flashed an animal's bite and hissed. Her canine teeth, long and curved, shined a halogen white.

"Shit! What the hell's wrong with you Amelia?" He said as he wiped the sleep from his eyes. "You've been reading those Harquins again."

"That's Harlequin," she said, and she had been. "and no I haven't."

Amelia turned, distancing herself from the bed. Her slender frame was long and taunt. It reminded him of a flame to a lit candle, and her voice struck him just as warmly.

"You want to have your way with me don't you?" Bob said as he studied the view she gave him. "As simple as that may appear, it just might be fun. It's like... cool."

Like a tempest, she turned on him, dipping

into huge subjects as she did peoples dark side's, the fear of loneliness, keeping ones pore's open to epic emotions. Her sarcasm always had to be strong, always extreme, and always passionate.

"Your use of the language is appalling." Amelia said." "Fun is not in my vocabulary. I have a problem being light when I mean no." She looked over her shoulder... "Bob. And cool is nowhere. I have no idea what that means because I am not someone cool. I'm someone who lives by instinct first, and not my brain. If fun is being crazy, to break the rules, to let in crazy thoughts, I like it. And there is no extension to this."

Bob just stared. Not only did her words go in one ear and out the other that was chalk board annoying, but he noticed his make shift coffin slash racing car bed needed a new coat of paint. With athletic physics, he leaped from his casket in one effortless bound. He circled her, smelling her luring scent and exhaled heartily.

"Humph." Bob said smartly.

He glanced at the six-foot-six grandfather clock that loomed over Amelia basically unconcerned with time. Bob walked up to the clock and wiped the oval face. If it wasn't for the quiet click of the pendulum it would have appeared to be broken and he knew it would cost dearly to repair it. Bob never worried about the costly amount of anything. It wasn't his clock, but its time struck him oddly. His own biological clock seemed out of tune also as if he were late for something. He stroked the face again.

"Is this the correct time Amelia?" Bob asked.

Like a tempest, mystery intact, was swept away by a slight smile covering a range of feelings from affection to malice. The Mona Lisa smug was like the coup de grace of her intimate philosophy. A bit of theory set aside to boggle his understanding, pilot his words to trip over themselves.

"Of course it is. The clock is in excellent working condition. So keep your hands to yourself." Amelia said.

"I don't understand. Either it's the butt-crack of dawn or this clock is broken." Bob said expressionless.

Without looking, Bob pointed up to a small hole in the skylight. The light lathered its way through a corner as if the ray were the business end of a flashlight, an effect that was unappreciated by Bob. Although the window darkened dramatically to any light, and brightened by night, it was still a worry to have but insisted upon by Amelia. The mosaic pane along the east stretch of the room was heavily tinted as well, and besides the skylight was the only other window in the apartment.

"Well?" He said stupidly, accompanied by a simpler yet awkward smirk.

Amelia's nose rose in the air as she spoke.

"If my immortal estimations mean anything to you," she said. "you'd leave it at that. Actually I'm hurt by your accusations and take immediate offense."

"But-" Bob clutched.

Amelia turned on him. Her Asian eyes, so persuading.

"Trust me." She said.

Calling her a liar or anything resembling the

word never sat well with Bob. The conversation was over, and to Bob it never happened.

"Lighten up shorty." He said reassuringly.

"What?" Amelia grimaced.

"That's a little thing I picked up from the home-boys in the hood." Bob said.

"Why do you insist on asking them inane questions?" Amelia said, her face still caught up in a questioning frown. "You're completely without reason."

Bob rubbed his smooth chin. "It's a man thing, Amelia." He said. "If I ever plan to get into those ancient panties of yours I have to learn what ever's up to romantic date." 'Besides, your dick will shrivel up and fall off,' the German vampire had told him. 'that's if you don't use it.' He added as a matter of fact.

Every now and then Bob, not sure, would grab his crotch to see if it was still there.

Amelia strapped on a black cloak trimmed in gold and gracefully turned. In that same motion, her cape swirled around her with a flare. She placed her hands on her hips, a pose to delegate a mood swing, causing her wrap to envelop her seductively and stared at Bob. A look many people mistook as charming.

"We do not love in such a disgusting manner. We are not real, and therefore sharing a common need take solace in just what we are: myth and legend, something to think about. Nothing more and nothing less." Amelia snapped sharply.

She threw her head back and ran a provocative tongue across her upper lip.

"Besides," Amelia said innocently. "how

do you know if I'm wearing panties?"

Bob's eyes brightened. "You're a teasing little..."

"Maybe." She shrugged with a huff.

"You've been playing with that tongue thing again." Bob said unsure of what effect the statement would have.

Amelia angled her head. "Maybe."

"I know what you're doing with it Amelia, and I think-"

"What. What do you think you perverted Neanderthal." Amelia interrupted. "You know nothing of the bond between this fallen angel and I. I knew of it before you, and I tell you that you have nothing to worry about. I am with you."

"But that flesh thing is still here isn't it?

Where is it this time, under the coffee table?"
Her eyes weakened. "In the medicine cabinet?
You told me you and that thing were history,
and that was four-hundred years ago. I throw
it out and somehow it comes back like a love
sick puppy." Bob recalled.

Amelia walked to the French windows
which raised two stories in mosaic pane and
threw them open with a wave of her hand.
They opened like the doors to a master study
gripped by an English butler.

The day had penetrated the dusk of the
apartment as if someone had flicked on a
switch. Bob leaped into the coffin, its lid
slamming and sealing him in. She glared at the
casket resentfully.

"Just deal with it." Amelia said flatly.

Bob's voice was a mere whisper. If you
turned your head a certain way the sound

would have been as distant as a conversation down a quiet street. "I heard that."

Amelia turned and leaped from the window. The French pane closed behind her. Bob continued to mumble through the closed casket. His words sounding as if his mouth was sewn shut, was unaware that she had already left.

Amelia circled a standing spruce. She dove beneath needles and cones and became a dream. A visual, suddenly unusual site, blending with nature and objects like a gaseous chameleon.

She grabbed the ends of her cape and surrounded her body in a parachute decent. The rush of cool air coming under her silk gown flushed her face and sent needles of ice through her private openings. The experience was a rush that tightened the bowels like a steep fall from a roller coaster ride, somehow needing and wanting more when once was not enough.

Her feet touched gravel but couldn't be heard. Amelia's ability to diffuse at will suddenly became a natural camouflage. Her sensitive hearing picked up music from a nightclub, an intense conversation about flowers from the floral shop next door, and lies over an intimate late lunch for two. The talk became heated as he told her how much he loved her, persuading her as Amelia imagined him raising the glass to his lips. Amelia breathed heavily dreaming that one day she too would be romanced or even lied to convincingly would be a switch. She flinched as if goosed and turned around.

"Bob!" Amelia said startled. "What are you doing out in the daylight?"

She held out her arms to catch him knowing from history that daylight would surely kill him, bring him to his knees screaming for shelter.

Bob reached inside his cape and pulled out a small bottle. Amelia crossed her arms, the concern wiped from her face.

"It's a bottle," Amelia said. "so what."

Bob smiled. "Look closer babe."

On the bottle, in small print, at the bottom read: extra strength sun block, Bob and Bob INC..

Amelia blinked. "Okay... I'll bite... what's in it?"

Bob cleared his throat. "Well, of course it's strictly top secret, and I could tell you but then I'd have to kill you."

"Spare me the details and get a real job... Robert." Amelia said roughly.

She spun on her heels and disappeared around the corner of the ally blending in with the All Hollows Eve treaters. This time the silence of an approaching presence was strong.

"And my name is Bob." He said through clinched teeth.

He turned to meet his victim. A man crazed in sweat held a sharp two foot spike aimed at Bob's heart. The victim, now predator stopped his attack in surprise.

"That looks like it might hurt doctor. And it looks awful heavy too. Mind if I relieve you of that tree branch?" Bob said with cesspool eyes.

Bob snatched it from his hand as the doctor turned and ran. His movements appeared motionless as if tip-toeing or slowly easing up on a person then stopping dead as if that film clip was to be edited. It was Bob who stopped his escape and was standing in front of the doctor as life-sized and as unreal as a picture from a dream.

"Why the rush doctor? Do I offend?" Bob said sarcastically.

Bob sniffed under both armpits. He read the doctor perfectly and grabbed him around his throat lifting the doctor off his feet. Bob drew him close, bringing the doctor within inches of his nose. He breathed into the doctors face and smiled brightly. Soon a pair of conical teeth appeared through the full smile and was the last thing Dr. Marcus D'Shay saw before he fainted.

Bob's mouth opened and his head tilted. Saliva dripped from the points of his canine teeth. A clatter of high pitched voices clashed with the on going traffic in the distance coming closer. The day was filled with mayhem. The kind of commotion he hid behind to quiet the screams that brought him so much pleasure. To drink the doctor dry and to stop his feeble attempts at his death was in his hands now. Bob, with amusement, threw him twenty feet into an open pile of trash.

Bob's eyes closed to mere slits. "Next time doctor, we'll have that lunch."

"Excuse me." A high pitched voice charged him from behind followed by mousy giggles. Bob's teeth retracted and he wheeled around. His eyes were glued; stuck to her breast protruding in mammoth declaration of milk potential, reaching out to the limits of a taunt low cut leather jacket. A short black leather skirt revealed a hint of leg where just enough eased over the lace of her thigh-high stockings. When he finally noticed her eyes they were blue. A clear, hot blue like the clean flame of an alcohol burner.

"Excuse me," The voice said again. "do you work around here?"

Bob's eyes focused. "No I don't." He said indirectly.

He squinted and looked again. There were two of them. Dressed identically. His eyes inadvertently dropped, but this time to the shorter of the two. Her skirt was an eyelash above the stockings and a hair above the hips and he could swear, to anyone who'd listen that you could almost see the pinch between her legs.

"You don't work around here but you're here... why, are you casing the joint or something?" The taller of the two asked.

Bob was becoming annoyed. "I'm sparing for roaches." He said. "Seen any?"

They giggled; harder.

"Yeah," The tall one said. "you might say we're experts on small cockroaches." She emphasized harshly on 'cock,' as they giggled and smiled.

At that moment shadows shifted around their feet. Too quick for the human eye. One of them was without this handicap, reached down, picked something up, and put it in his mouth. He watched them closely as he chewed, staring right through them. He heard the short one swallow and the other's stomach gurgle as if she were about to vomit. He could almost sense the sour taste of bile at the back of her throat. It wouldn't be long before she'd reel over and up-chuck her earlier meal. He'd make his move then. Knock the short one unconscious and demonically take his time with the other.

He swallowed and cautiously looked discretely over their shoulders. There was another ally behind them going North and South. They were in an ally pointing East and West with yet another behind Bob spilling out the same as the one behind the two women. The buildings were tall with brick and masonry blocks. Tin and steel garbage cans with tons of refuge spilling over their edges gave it graze-land quality for any stray. It was perfect.

Screams, if any, would be muffled. They'd bounce off the walls and shoot ice needles through his body. His eyes bulged as the thought of taking life eased down his throat.

"Nice parlor trick Houdini." The tall one

said as she stepped closer, then jumped back. A scream caught in her throat and the muscles to her bladder tightened as her heart quickened its beat. A crunch so familiar, so eerie echoed through her entire body. She wanted to spit the taste from her mouth, erase the thought from her mind and start the day over again. She wondered if he knew. If he could feel her struggle for control as she eased a quiet sigh, a normal breath as if everything was all right.

His voice was definite. "That's Bob."

She was staring and felt it and wondered if it was as obvious to him. She wanted to continue to appear at ease scrapping her foot gently across the concrete as she looked squarely into Bob's face.

He's weird but interesting she thought, her mind also washing away the grasp of that cockroach she knew she stepped on and the one she knew, or thought, he did or didn't eat.

"Come on," she said, forcing a calm demeanor, beckoning with her outstretched hand. "buy us a drink honey."

"That's Bob." He said again.

"And by the way," She said as she wiggled her fingers stretching her arm to its limit. "nice costume."

Bob looked himself over. "Thanks."

He walked up to her. Their hands touching, and their eyes locking.

"So, what line of work are you in?" She asked.

Bob froze looking at the shorter of the two wondering why she never spoke and just what would keep this chick from yakking. He had to think quickly.

"I paint the white stripes in the middle of the street." He said.

Bob's eyes shifted from one to the other. That wasn't what he wanted to say but that's what came out.

A detailed image of the bottom of the doctor's feet hung over large plastic garbage bags while his body was slumped somewhere beneath empty boxes and other trash was distracting enough.

"I've always wanted to know who did that." The taller of the two said.

They clutched Bob's arms and when the first step was taken the short one spoke and continued to talk in the highest squealing tone he had ever heard. It became clear why she wouldn't allow herself to speak unless she was walking. The constant dragging of her heels and swaying of her hips would take anyone's mind off her garrulous squawking.

She was teasingly simple. Her legs were skinny that made them look long and she walked as if the two inch heels were a part of her. Her nose, aristocratic but too blade-like to be considered attractive, in fact was tremendously out of context with her bold painted lips and clear brown eyes.

Bob interrupted at the only moment he could. He wanted to stop the reeling seduction of Amelia from playing over and over in his mind.

The two women took in a deep breath as if to continue taking, with Bob, in their lapse, agreeing to the place mentioned: The Hangman's Noose. They looked at him wide-eyed trying to remember if in fact they mentioned such a place. Bob knew of the place because it had no mirrors.

The one glanced questionably at the other and they both shrugged their shoulders awkwardly.

They walked past a dozen places packed to the front door with people before the conversation picked up again, with Bob drawn up in reverie, and the two not waiting on an answer of certainty just waged on about one thing or another. One would giggle as the other asked a question or went back several years to remember when was how she put it.

"What was the name of that place again sweetie?"

"That's Bob. Bob's my name. BOB! B-O-B, BOB." He said agitated.

The taller of the two eyes had brightened

as if shot but only gave a mordant interpretation in pantomime.

"Oh, is that your name or is that what you do?" She said.

She began to bob her head up and down like a dashboard dog. Her tongue pushed out against her cheek making faces to emphasize a point. Bob had a few facial expressions of his own. His immediate look was one that would make Captain Kirk gag as if he just inhaled an alien pubic hair. 'I don't see the logic in that Jim.' Spock would say giving him a slap across the back of the neck as if that would prevent sudden hysteria. 'Are you out of your Vulcan mind?' Doctor McCoy would ask.

Again, they giggled and Bob wanted to slap them both still hearing off in the distant reaches of his mind; 'Are you out of your Vulcan mind? 'Be patient with them.'

Somehow their laughter was uplifting, partly because it stopped them from talking.

They continued walking past brightly colored mercury vapor lights. Although quite talkative and dizzy-minded, the two women appeared to know where they were going.

Bob was the first to point out the Hangman's Noose that was sandwiched between the Watering Hole, and the Resting Place. Bob entered first. The scene was mellow with numerous clean shaven men and peroxide ladies. The style ultra-contemporary with white vaulted arches, marble steps and arched doorways. Tall pillars floated off the crystal waxed floors like some kind of midnight fantasy boat ride by the sea.

Bob was ushered to the bar where two stools like cupped hands stood idyll at its rim. He threw out his hands like the maître d' of a restaurant. "Please." The two women looked at one another again as they sat and giggled with a hunch of a shoulder and a tilt of a hand. They had been making roundabout insinuations since they picked him up. Soon he'd make a few of his own and wondered politely just how much predominant influence would break the monotony.

Bob motioned for the bartender with a bow of his head and a raise of his finger. A cleaver move he'd seen so many times on cable.

The bartender's large fingers, swollen as if submerged in water for hours, clutched a terry-cloth towel. He wiped the black teak counter and with three fingers of his other hand dipped them into two hand-painted rim aquavit glasses. When the slender tubes vanished underneath the counter it was wiped clean and replaced by two coasters. He gave Bob the house smile that was as dull as his caffeine stained teeth. He was bald with a fringe of gray hair around the back of his head. His face was plump and rosy and he had the placid, satisfied manner of a pastor of a wealthy congregation. He had large warm eyes that looked like they belonged to a cocker spaniel puppy. They opened wide as he asked Bob what was his pleasure. Again he wiped the counter like in an old T.V. western.

"I'll have a champagne split and the scrambling of a long island ice tea, not stirred, not shaken, just over the rocks and hold the umbrella. And a Jack Daniel's neat." Bob said happily.

"Will there be anything else?" The bartender asked.

"You can give me a drink while I'm

waiting." Bob said.

He gave Bob a muddled expression. Bob just looked away.

From the ladies' conversation he made note of the tall ones' name; Lisa. The delicate way her hair blew free in the breeze and gently across the profile of her face, inclined upward toward the darkening sky. Of course the part about being a mindless slut when drunk was pieced together from thrown hints here and there by her diminutive friend was another stirring feature he craved into memory.

The sounds of Phil Collins, Groovy Kind of Love blended in with the closing good-byes of the Miami Sound Machines, It Cuts Both Ways. The melodies soothed him. It was stilted at first-in a crowd, men and women standing in comfortable little groups with glasses in their hands, talking your usual crap.

There was also something trite yet pleasing in a roundabout way. And there it was.

Her smell eau de perfect. She was twenty feet away but Bob picked up her scent like a blood hound in search of an escaped prisoner. A blood hound, Bob imagined, and then his mind began to drift. Dreamy visions of her wafted into his mind.

She was a tall attractive blond with curves in places where some women don't even have places. Dressed in a black clinging dress; appearing to be in her vigorous 20's. She projected the aura of being the ultimate party girl in Chicago, her idea of fun was to fuck until the cows come home. As she smiled, she would let her gorgeous face and figure do most of the talking. Bob insisted on a bit of blood in exchange for a good lay. She agreed.

Bob made a small incision on her wrist and

slowly sucked blood from the open wound. He wanted to make the initial cut on the lower belly, just below the panty line where it wouldn't show but it was the wrist or nothing and Bob was hungry.

After a good long drink he licked the cut closed. She wasted no time unzipping his pants and pulling them down to his knees. She pushed him back on the bed and pulled up her skirt. She stood over him and managed to wedge his firm body between her legs. The ritual went slowly as she made grinding, circular motions with her hips until finally she was filled with him. The muscles in her body tensed until she saw Bob's eyes close. She continued to make small grinding circles with her hips. She teased him as if he were cheap labor called in-in mist of pruning the hedges around her twenty acre home. She began to scoot up then back, circulating her hips and muscles in a steady rhythm. She pulled the shoulders of her dress down her arms and over her wrist. She scooting up along the sensitive parts of his body then pushing back aggressively. She pumped and grind feverishly, unaware that Bob had taken one of her ample breast into his mouth. The sensation was explosive and Bob closed his eyes, envisioning his sweating body trimming the hedges and her naked breast, bobbing as she called from an open window. "Hernandez... Hernandez...."

Faintly the words sounded more and more like... Bob. Then came the nudge, and the fidelity of reality.

"Bob, here's your drink." The shorter of the two said politely.

He took it eagerly and brought the glass to his lips. Figures began to block his view of the woman he had been fantasizing about. He backed off, looking into the Waterford glass that appeared to be full of straight whiskey. He decided just to take a sip, and he did.

The woman turned into view. Her aquiline nose made Bob back off the glass again. He took another sip to be sure. The scent now was eau de bow-wow. He took the shot and it went down smoothly. He placed the empty glass on the counter between the two women he had come in with. The bartender was slow in reacting so Bob decided to hold a conversation with one of his new found friends. She held his stare disdainfully, making it obvious to him that their tete-a-tete was interrupted by Bob's fill er' up again gesture. Politely and almost intimidating, she blushed and shied away.

Lisa tapped Bob on the shoulder. She was

huddled over a long island ice tea blending the mixture together with a finger.

"Excuse me, Lisa right?" Bob asked pointing a finger from his temple directly towards her as if he pulled that vital information from his memory files.

"That's right." Lisa said. "I don't remember telling you my name."

An inner voice spoke as Bob's mind whirled. 'Lisa, you have a three inch hair growing next to your right nipple. Where did that come from?' Bob thought wildly. 'Watch your thoughts; they become words.' The inner voice said.

Bob's lips parted. Unable to speak, he put it to thought again.

'Watch your words; they become actions.' The voice said. 'Well then, if I can't say anything what should I do?' Bob thought. 'Watch your actions Bob; they become habits.' The voice churned. 'I have but few habits.' Bob pushed. 'Watch your habits; they become character.' The inner voice said calmly. 'Watch your character; it becomes your destiny.' The voice fading in and out.

"So... are you ovulating?" Bob asked.

His voice was deep and breathe warm. The spell took its course as Lisa, finger in glass, sat as if contemplating an appropriate answer to his question, or maybe she didn't know what ovulating was.

"What'll ya' have?" The bartender asked brusquely as if recklessly fed up with having to baby-sit alcoholics.

He was short on manners but Bob receded and named his poison.

"Bourbon. Neat." Bob said.

The bartender pulled a bottle of Jack Daniel's with a pour spout from underneath the counter. Bob put his hand over the Waterford glass and nodded a dislike towards his choice. Bob pointed to a unique hand blown bottle housed in a glass case. It was fifteen years old of the establishment finest, and Bob wanted nothing less.

"A shot of that is pretty expensive." The bartender noted bluntly.

"Then keep them coming till' my hat floats." Bob said with a convincing chill.

Bob released his grip and from the corner of his eye he could see the fatty part of the bartenders' cheeks return to its natural eraser blush.

Bobs' senses became aware of treated

meats. A buffet was seated in the corner and if you're an authority on raw bologna and wilting lettuce, this was the place to be.

Hushed murmurs mingled well with the soft spoken words of Patty Smyth: Sometimes love ain't enough, as Bob shook his head as a matter of fact.

By midnight the casual academic talk would be replaced by more interesting subjects-the Bulls, what's a person like you doing in a place like this and that all time favorite, have you had a good screw lately.

A woman opened her mouth wide and bit into the huge sandwich she was holding. A gooey sauce, the color and texture of a stallions' semen squirted between her fingers and she licked it off her hand casually. She caught him looking at her and tipped him a wink. Bob lifted his glass from the bar and raised his drink in a polite barrel-house salute. He returned back to the women and settled his dusty loafers on the bar stools' foot rest. Lisa placed a hand on Bob's crotch and gave it a squeeze.

"Hello! Is that a tree trunk in your pocket or are you just happy to see me?" Lisa asked hopefully.

"It's your guess Lisa." Bob said embarrassed.

Her sour drink was almost empty and still she stirred the tart mixture with her finger. She squealed as if pinched and pulled her finger from the glass. The tempting potion glistened under the faint lights as she pressed the serum from her hand. The cut was clean and her look, magnetic as she sat slightly hunched with a salaciously flushed face. Her life source fell slowly to its death. Bob almost fainted at the lose of the life giving venom. His mouth watered and his palms started to sweat. He could feel the heat rising to the top of his head as a bead of perspiration trickled laterally the length of his sideburns.

"Here, let me." Bob said.

He employed pressure with his tongue and sucked lightly. After several seconds he took advantage of the moment and applied some reality.

He darted his tongue between her fingers letting the blood nursing tentacles of his tongue massage the web of her hand. Feeling somewhat nervous, letting her thoughts form images of something not present, Lisa closed her legs. She jumped slightly. Lisa tried to stray from fancying the suggestion but in fact was modeling the actual experience and the person involved was Bob. His hand between her legs and under her skirt rubbing the amateur parts of her orifice. She opened her legs unknowingly letting the tight leather skirt raise just above her hips. The act went unnoticed as their eyes fixed on each other.

Bob pulled hard, sucking the blood from the open wound. A rush came over him. She placed a hand over his, applying a gentle squeeze as if to say 'no, stop... another time, another place.' As the blood drained from the cut, she gripped his hand tighter, drawing in short breaths through her nose followed by a puppy whine as if needing to feed. Bob took his hand away as the scene became a frenzy of tight lipped indulgences. She pampered her craving by pulling her skirt down, letting her hands run the length of her thighs. She shook off a chill and began to rub her legs together. Her eyes were no longer tranquil cool blue. They were suggestive and naughty.

"Let's step out around back and take a look at that swollen gland of yours." Lisa said almost breathlessly.

Bob offered his hand and Lisa stepped down from the bar stool. Before leaving, the bartender asked Bob to settle the tab. He approached the bar with a stern look and pounded the lacquer top twice with his fist. It made the bartender jump as if he were trying to hide something. Bob smiled and opened his hand. Inside Bob's palm was a one-hundred dollar bill that the bartender took quickly and scurried away like a roach sensing light. They left the other nursing a champagne split from a flute-shaped bubbly glass.

***

Meanwhile, Doctor Marcus D'Shay walked

down a hall brushing the clinging stench from his clothes. He walked up to a door marked 531 B and pressed his left palm on the wall. A panel fell outward exposing red, green, and white flashing lights. It was a picture perfect outlay of a hand with a sensor slot from the base of the palm to the index finger. Doctor Marcus took out his press card, sliding it through the sensor slot, causing the elevator doors to open. He walked inside and turned around just as the doors closed. The elevator jerked and made an upward movement. It stopped with a whine. The doors opened and he walked down a long hall and into the main suite. The silence was almost deafening. Although several stories up, the wall, and the floors were soundproof. And for additional privacy, double-glaze tinted windows. The place seemed set in a sort of vacuum. The feeling crept in that if you listened to the silence long enough, it would become hard to breathe.

"Thank God for central cooling." Marcus said quietly to himself.

Still something was out of place. He looked up and down the wood paneling of the spacious apartment and noticed the blinds halfway shut.

Bands of light from a street lamp came through the green-tinted windows. The entire room was decorated in a horizontal underwater pinstripe. It made the living room strangely alien, and it suddenly occurred to him that something was missing. He walked further into the center of the room. Several hidden detectors had already picked him and identified him, in the other room as well as here, but a monitor in the wall above a thirty-four inch HDTV, wide screen picture receiver wasn't satisfied. It beeped and printed up:

THE OCCUPANT OF THIS APARTMENT IS NOT AVAILABLE. THIS IS A POLICED UNIT. PLEASE IDENTIFY YOURSELF BY IMITATING THE CORRECT ACCESS CODE OR LEAVE IMMEDIATELY. IF YOU FAIL TO LEAVE OR IDENTIFY YOURSELF, A TEN SECOND WARNING WILL BE GIVEN, FOLLOWING WHICH THE DOORS AND WINDOWS WILL LOCK AUTOMATICALLY, AND A GASEOUS POISON WILL FILL EACH ROOM... REPEAT: THIS IS A POLICED UNIT.

Feeling unjustifiably aggressive towards the machine, and a bit annoyed, he did nothing but waited. After a count of three the screen wiped itself clean and spoke aloud through the wireless speakers around the apartment repeating the same instructions in several different languages.

"Bridgette," Marcus shouted over the verse in French.

He walked over to a desk that sat in front of a window looking out over Lake Michigan. He pulled the flex-rest keyboard from underneath the rim of the desk and it angled slightly away from him. He ran his fingers across the bottom row of buttons, pushed delete and looked at the monitor screen.

"TEN SECOND WARNING COMMENCES NOW... TEN... NINE... EIGHT..."

"This is ridiculous..."**Bridgette!**" He shouted in the machines lapsed silence.

"SEVEN..."

He turned quickly and began punching in a

series of numbers.

"FIVE..."

The doctor slammed the desk with his fist and tried again.

"THREE..."

He turned to the monitor screen and screamed,: "BRIDGETTE." The sound went through every opened room but came back unanswered. He dashed around an end table and ran down the hall placing both hands on the wall that lead to the elevator.

The edges of the door inflated cutting off any escape of the poisonous gas. Behind him doors locked and sealed with the same vacuum like effect. He dove to the floor as if a frag grenade had landed inches in front of him.

Again, the silence.

***

Lisa physically dragged Bob out into the alley. She pushed him in between a wall and garbage can. She looked down and knelt in front of him. Lisa rubbed his thighs and ran her tongue up the crotch of his pants. Bob was curious and took no pleasure in her taunting, but never-the-less watched in silence. Lisa unzipped his pants and reached in. She fumbled around for a moment and Bob, chilled by her touch, shivered. At first grasp she thought she found what she was looking for and pulled with excitement. Her tongue lengthened over her bottom lip, and her eyes brightened ravishingly. She pulled it out, almost stabbing herself in the eye and fell back.

"Hey, what kind of cruel joke is this? There's a law ya' know." Lisa said firmly.

"What do you mean?" Bob asked.

Lisa stood, dusting herself off in the process. She held the stick out with a sardonic look on her face.

"This is a stick man. What's it doing in your pants?" She asked.

"Beats the hell out of me." Bob said.

"I ought to beat you with it. You probably prefer this to a woman anyway." She said sharply.

"Why don't you take another look at it my lady." Bob answered coolly.

His eyes were mesmerizing as her face went blank. He pinched a vein in her throat with the tip of his nails. Before she fell, he was drinking her blood from the wound. His jaws like vice-grips kept her on her feet. As the blood drained, she began to wilt. The spike fell from her hand as she softly touched him around his waist. A moan escaped her mouth that fascinated him beyond mortal fantasies. He held her and drank lovingly. His hands moved against the curves of her back then down to the hill of her buttocks. Bob squeezed with curious passion. She accepted him weakly and was lifted by his strong arms.

She moaned faintly as her hands left his body. He let her fall to the ground like a ribbon held up by the wind. Bob looked down at her body and from the soft veil of shadows he heard a voice.

"You called for me my love."

"I called for you not my love." Bob whispered.

"The words to which you only have for me echoed off the stars into my heart this All Hollows Eve. Did you not call into the winds, the words, my lady?" The voice said.

He raised his head and looked into a corner where the setting sun created a deep shadow. His mouth open and his lips pouted stumbled for words and found none. His eyes pierced through milky illusions to behold her stare. The stare that sent him back a thousand years to their first meeting. A faint winged whisper was heard and he knew he was in trouble.

She wouldn't understand how a woman's blood compared to men gave him a completely different sensation. Maybe it had something to do with him being a virgin when adapted into this cult. That was stupid he thought. It was the kill that made his blood boil there and the soft whispers in his ear from his female victims that encouraged decades of habit. "Take me, please take me." They would beg. Going against the code of his brethren, he obliged them willingly. 'In a hundred years or so your thing will just shrivel up and fall off,' Mikhail would say. 'That's if you don't use it.' She'd never understand.

Bob walked back to the bar in search for answers to his quest. The Monster Mash was blaring over the speakers. He cloaked his body and walked through the crowd like a shadow through fog. He stepped up to her.

"I have questions for you," he said in a tone so serious it was weird for even him.

"Let's dance." She said gleefully.

She grabbed him by the hand and started to dance inches from their seats. Bob looked at her wayward motions as another chorus of Monster Mash spilled from the sound system.

Bob timidly bounced up and down, then from side to side. He feathered his cape in front of his face, spun on his heels and bent over in a wiggling motion. He disappeared from the crowd as he bent and shimmied to the music. The song died out and the crowd clapped as if on cue. Bob stood strikingly upright, turned and snatched the woman from the room. They went to the lower level where the music was calmly mid-sixties. Bob spun the girl around, looked into her eyes and she sat down.

"That worked." He said to himself, surprised. "I have questions for you."

"About what Bob." She said in a robotics tone.

Bob smacked her and brought his question to her again.

"I have a question, about women." Bob

asked frantically.

"Are you out of your Vulcan mind?" She said.

"What?" Bob asked.

"I said, are you out of your freakin mind; that hurt. You didn't have to slap me. I'll do whatever you want." She said with the charm and vocal clarity of a school girl.

"It's about women. I want to know the mutual fantasy they all share. The one they dare bring to light. It's hidden somewhere in their bodies and minds. It has something to do with the no that rolls from their lips and the moaning yes in their eyes. It's so confusing." Bob said seriously.

"Damn Bob, you're deep. Where's my girlfriend, and how come you don't call me by my name?" She asked curiously.

Again Bob look deep into her eyes.

"What is your name?" Bob asked as if interested.

"Candy." She said happily.

"Figures." Bob smirked.

He stared deep and took great pleasures in commanding her to perform acts on her body. A little something for him and a little something for her. A crowd gathered and Bob gave them a still, sharp look that made them coward away.

"What is the answer to my question, Candy?" Bob asked, left eyebrow rose.

He wanted to deal with these mortals without the powers within his soul. He knew they couldn't lie and would do whatever he asked, but strangely enough, American women were curious to the difference and would perform odd rituals just by the asking. After sucking her thumb, pulling it in and out of her mouth as if auditioning for a porno flick, he knew she was his.

"Take me. All I want is to be taken by you." Candy said soothingly.

"That's not quite the answer I was looking for." Bob said with a frown. "Tell me what I need to know for this may be my last-"

"I want to be taken by a man who knows what he wants," Candy interrupted. "pulled into his grasp, not weakening to my timid denials. I want strength in his pursuance of my femininity. Be gentle with me, but take me like the beast that possesses your desires. I want to be taken and made to submit, lovingly; hungrily."

She stood and stared into Bob's eyes with the same defying tease as... as... Amelia. Yes, the surety struck him like a round house slap.

3

On Friday [October 30] Amelia paced back
and forth against the hardwood floors.
Shaving a groove into the tarnished wood, she
threw fits and threats into the air.

"He's still the same." Amelia raved. "How
could he? He'll never change. Always craving
the distasteful reactions and babbling's of

those mortal wenches. And to call that bitch the same name he vowed as to chant to me only. That pathological lying son-of-a-bitch! I'd kill him if it wasn't for the fact he was already dead. And the whore too for that matter. At every turn he pushes me."

She stomped towards the coffee table pushing it aside with a strong stroke of an arm. Amelia bowed in a sadistic prayer over the shallow hole. She removed the soiled rag from its socket, unfolded it gently and placed the smooth flesh in her lap. It lay between her legs, warm and limp. She stroked at its wrinkles. It began to move like an awakening new born. She gripped it in both hands, rubbing it with promises within an Aladdin's lamp. The serpent's tongue, in its full erection, flexed a full seven inches, then hardened. She rubbed it against her face, passing it across her lips, and kissed it.

She threw the serpent's tongue across the room. It banked off the wall and onto the floor. It rolled back to her and fell into its grave.

A tear rolled down her cheek, setting her back a distance in time.

She was of a careless age with repressed sexual fantasies, and he, that fine young gentleman, smiling energetically, full of life and ideas. Humph; she thought.

She was crying one day and as he walked up beside her he reached over and dried her tears. It was a normal reaction to look up, to thank the person who showed such sensitivity. Her eyes were fixed on the impressions left behind in the dry dirt. She looked down to his feet and saw hooves. She perceived it to be the Devil.

She was sure that her general mood had

invited the Devil's attention in the first place. She wasn't stupid, she was far from that or so she thought. She just needed someone.

Sitting back on her legs she recalled the many years of knowing him fully. He became the object of her oedipal wishes.

She would delay coming home from school until it was dark... and he would be there. Appearing from nowhere as if she thought him up.

As a young man his sexual appearances were pleasing, even gentle. The years and his callings became jaded, and his form took on shapes that drove her to surrender under a bed of wool sack and straw. He would laugh and scorn her maliciously.

In a fortnight he appeared again carrying a book, written with blood, of covenants made by others with him. His voice was deep and soothing as he urged her to add her own name. It seemed to Amelia that he had but one central purpose, he wished to gain a new follower for his infamous cult. Amelia refused.

The Devil struck her, sending her frail body to the dirt and straw floor. He breathed fire from his mouth, burning away the timid threads of clothing that sagged against her body. Again, as incubus, they feasted on flesh and indiscriminate intercourse. She wished to be rid of him but didn't know how.

Again he presented himself and desired of her blood, and she would have done it, but wanted a knife for reasons that she could not conceal from him. The knife was denied and again he asked her to sign the book.

The Devil was using every means, including physical torture to break down her defenses. As a means of persuasion, he mixed offers of gifts and favors with threats and actual violence. In exchange for commitment he would give to her such things that would suit her youthful fancy, including: money, silks, fine clothes, ease from labor, or to show her the world. She refused.

Upon this he displayed an unnatural temper, arising from the foulness of the stomach and corruptness of her blood, occasioning visions in her brain and strange fantasies.

He promised her charms and potions to alter the course of peoples' lives who could harm her. He explained in detail the results her touch, her look, her words could cause and would cause, if she signed. Again she refused and again he forced her to commit sexual obscenities upon his body, then he struck her again, and again.

One night, deep within the forest surrounding which is now called the Bald Mountains in Germany, near Kiev, another argument took shape but this time, Amelia wavering to submit to the covenant by signing the book.

A rustle of leaves distracted their quarreling. Faint tremors as if running on cold soil echoed rhythmically distant as a heartbeat through the air. Then a hardy thud followed by silence. The Devil disappeared. Amelia ran to the root of the source. She found, laying in the autumn leaves, a man in matted black. His face was a shaded opaque. His age hidden behind closed eyes. His hair, a blaring sandy brown flowed like a flame from a match around his head. She knelt beside him, touching his brow. A look of soft concern suffused her face as her touch did nothing to awaken him. She touched his cheek and just as soothingly closed her eyes reciting a wish. A chill touched her flesh and she shook it off. She opened her eyes and was greeted by the hazel stare of her patient.

"Twenty," she said lightheartedly.

"What?" He asked through blurry eyes. "You're an age of twenty or so years," she explained.

They gazed into each other's eyes for what seemed an eternity. At once, they were standing. He held her in his arms as if they had done this a thousand times. His touch made her skin flush with color and her eyes sparkled like sapphires embedded in pearls. Her lips were full and encouraging. They reached for a kiss. Amelia's eyes closed, her arms embraced his broad shoulders but the kiss never came. A telltale puncture mark, right where legend said they'd be was left as he raised his head. A feeling she had never experienced or dreamed of seemed to lift her into a spiral of sudden emotions. She sighed tiredly. Her breasts swelled, and she tightened her grip around his neck. Her legs parted as she lifted herself onto him. His hands moved to her back, then to her shoulders where he unceremoniously pulled her from his body. Her eyes shot brilliance.

"Who are you?" She begged. "Your demure is so tantalizingly strange."

"I am yours my lady, and now you are mine. But I must bid you a fond adieu." He lowered his head in a bow.

He placed her feet on solid ground and bowed again. He held her hand to his lips, and kissed it.

"When will I see you again, and what shall I call you?" She inquired.

"You will call me, uhh... Bob!" He replied with uncertainty.

"Bob. What an odd name." She said confused.

A dim bead of light pierced through the trees gracing his forehead. He turned swiftly and momentarily stood chanting in a grieving whisper, "I love you."

A thrust of air pushed Amelia off her feet. She gracefully landed on her backside with arms thrown behind her. She reached out to him. Rays of light warmed her arms and face. He was gone. She looked up through the stretch of trees and colors. The words: my lady, touched her and made her heart feel twice its size. Amelia spoke softly; as it, for the moment, was the only thing she could say.

It was... good-bye.

The Devil's book slammed to the dirt of broken sticks and rusted leaves. Had he been watching? Her mind raged.

She fingered the cover of the book and pushed it away. Amelia lifted herself and spoke into the air.

"I will make a deal with you Lucifer." She said with spirit.

The ground opened emitting a foul and cruel stench. From its depth, the Prince of darkness appeared in its beastly glory.

"And what pact is this?" Satan spoke in I and thou differentiation.

"I seek the configurations of youth." She said without looking at him.

Satan laughed so loud and hard, trees

snapped at its volatility.

"And what will you do for me?" Satan asked.

"I will bring others to coven with you. Wives to sit by your side at each Sabbath." Amelia said sternly.

The Devil looked around.

"This is all too amusing Amelia." The Devil said calmly. "I will agree to this pact. For a thousand years, you shall act at my behest bringing me such luxuries as you've mentioned. Behold at your feet."

Amelia looked down at the tips of her sandals. There, a small round compact and a soiled rag lay idle. She picked the two packages up with curiosity, and fingered them lightly. Amelia unfolded the rag and the stench of putrid death stung her nose. She did not flinch, as she was accustomed and hardened by the Devil's deceits.

"And what are these strange rituals you've laid before me?" Amelia asked.

"The serpents tongue you now fondle will cast a familiar shadow when summoned by the word: BENEDICITE." The Devil explained. "Upon this, I will come and take you for my pleasure. If not summoned I will shadow you at every full moon until it breaks and take you as I please. The exposed plate is your own vanity. Care for it well."

Her psychic configurations were granted. Claims of omnipotent strength and irresistible beauty, an internal figure of perfection. The transference developed in a mirror to form two people. She could escape the usual constrains of body and mind, and obtain powers literally supernatural. Her words, her touch, her look were directly and destructively, efficacious. The serge that supplied her drive energies contributed to her libidinal tensions. Her other being, her inner self as an independent person took hold of the flesh nightly to tame her libido. She did not treat it as her first step of action, let alone as a love object. In fact, there was no clear hint of erotic aims.

Years came and went, yet she could not find her dawn lover and her conduct with the serpents tongue was to throw a cloud over her little ménage a trios.

Amelia soon found that her winged suitor was a creature of the night of many a soul and fell trapped again in his arms never to leave. The moment of that recurring twist at daybreak never came and so often Amelia returned to the callings of the warm flesh.

Bob had come to her one night and found Amelia soaked in foul sweat. Her legs were widened as if conceiving a child and the stiffened tongue lay beside her. Her eyes exposed to the candle light surrounding her bed gave way to a look of greed and passion. Her panting and soft seductive ravings somehow intrigued him. Her eyes forever holding his at bay tried to summon the occurrence with just one look. The act became a frenzy of rubbing, thumping, and howling. She moved her free hand to her stomach, then to her breast where she cupped it in her warm palm and squeezed as if relieving a pain. Her eyes closed and her hips moved vigorously. Bob didn't know what to do. Her appetite for this effectual wand was unwavering. It was his princess and he knew that a need such as this would have to be controlled by his hand, but he didn't know what to do.

She grabbed the hardened flesh in her fist performing rude acts like a carpenter forcing in a nail with a twelve-ounce hammer. Amelia hissed and screamed at the top of her lungs flashing a canine bite. Bob had thought it done, but she pulled the flesh from its nest and rubbed it across her body and face. She licked and stroked it clean placing it teasingly again, beside her.

For several hundred years his sole quest was to uncover the secrets to effeminate pleasures. For several hundred years, she waited. A diabolical temper building, then changing course as she, at points, needed to confront the flesh.

Tonight, again, the fluid builds.

Amelia dug the flesh from the hole and parted her legs. She rubbed the flesh against her thigh and it hardened quickly. Her breathing came in short gasps as a dream like figure of Bob took seed in her mind. Again she flung the flesh to the floor.

"I am so ill of you," she claimed. "and I wish to nullify the entire agreement."

In a blink of an eye, the hoofed creature stood before Amelia. Its tail weighing every ton it seemed, slammed to the floor. Amelia looked up and the Devil, standing twelve feet into the air with shoulders, arms, and legs just as extending, smiled. A curious mist fogged the room from his bowels and mouth. The book fell from this mist and opened to a page craved from flesh.

"Sign the book." Satan said soothingly.

"I've served you for nearly a millennia." Amelia grasped. "Isn't that enough?"

This enraged the Devil and so he struck

her with a single swipe of his hand and sent Amelia flying into the dark, dusty mist of the large room.

"Sign the book, witch." Which sounded more like the derivative of wicce.

Amelia came stomping through the water cloud, hands marching at her side. She walked up to the Devil and with clenched fist struck Satan in his groin. The Devil doubled over with an angry moan. She balled both hands tight, closed her eyes and without touching him struck out with both arms sending him twisting into the veiled fog.

Not a sound came back from the dark corners. The silence; chilling. Questions came back unanswered as she backed up to take cover. Backing up was a crime of thought, and she, Amelia, retreated into the powerful grip of Satan. He picked her up and threw her against a wall. Her body fixed, imprinted into dry wall and oak plywood.

"Why don't you just go... leave!" She pleaded.

The Devil approached her, raining the sounds of a thousand Clydesdales beneath his feet. He gripped Amelia's face between two twisted fingers and roared.

"Sign the book!!" He screamed at her.

Amelia wasn't worried by this, but fear was indeed her enemy tonight. She was sarcastic in any weather and he would have to produce a great deal more to get her to sign.

"Okay, take as much time as you need. No hurry." She said calmly.

The Devil pulled his arm back and like a forked branch, gouged his fingers around Amelia's body and pulled her from the wall.

Cakes of brick and plaster fell like an avalanche to the floor. He squeezed her body with thundering pounds of pressure and brought her close to his mouth. Her arms hung loose around his satanic grip. Amelia's head showing the only signs of life raised to greet the black soul-less eyes of Satan. His nostrils flared, spilling lime green toxin from every pore onto the hardwood floor. It sizzled then settled to a corrosive stain.

"That's going to be hell to get out. Do you have any idea what a woman goes through cleaning up after you?" Amelia said sarcastically.

He raised her above his head and slammed her to the floor. Dust rose and the mist swirled around her body. As the tainted fog cleared, Satan looked down at her sprawled figure. Not a hint of makeup was smeared, and not a bruise visible as Amelia wet her lips and opened her eyes. She raised an arm to wipe the dust from her face and noticed a chipped nail. She pointed up to the Devil with blood-shot eyes.

"Your ass is out now you arrogant bastard!" Amelia said directly.

She slammed her hand to the floor. Before she could rise, the Devil assaulted her and sat on her breast. The weight took the breath and almost the life from Amelia. He forced her to view the hellish shapes of more devils than anyone had ever seen in the world. In his persistent treatment of her, he dove his hand into her mouth, reaching and driving further into her soul with murderous intent.

The French windows blew open and a gust of wind from the heights cleared the mist. Amelia laid gagging and clutching her throat to find relief. She sat up, jerking her head from side to side. The room had been clear of his dimensions. She ran a stiff hand through her hair and wiped the corners of her eyes. The wind was cold and unyielding. She picked herself figuratively out of a ditch and floated to the window. With bent eyes she recalled the events and closed the window with a clutch of her hand as if grabbing at ones collar. She turned swiftly around to capture what the shadows hid. A thump came from behind her. Amelia's senses dull.

'Who would make such a noise,' she thought. 'Surely not Satan.'

Amelia stepped away from the window then turned to meet it. She angled her head as if in thought and snapped her fingers. The French windows opened dramatically. She was stunned at what she saw in the window's avenue.

4

The curse of a thirteenth hour would come slowly this eve as the malignant strain of dying, doleful groans like bitter music ejaculated from a plight, a condition so premature, that romance this night as many people knew of them, would still be based on techniques of the past. If it weren't for knightly adventures and supernatural occurrences in long-ago times and far away places, romantics would be as passé as a prelude to a kiss.

In the mist of myth and legend, men were only concerned about their bravery on the field of battle, not the proper department at court and castle.

But somehow inspired by love, reflected an inspiring preoccupation with formal conduct. In addition to courage in knightly combats, most heroes acquired differences to the social class of women. The result was a code of ethics that made love an ennobling ideal-a conception that has been one of the distinguishing marks of male heroism.

In the wake of battles, bodies would be flung carelessly like a bachelor's dirty laundry.

The screams of senescent crushed bones, torn ligaments, and gouged larynx could no longer be concealed by the mayhem of the crowd that stood in awe at dozens of mangled relenting carcasses.

A man lay hemorrhaging, the blood bubbling from his cardinal stained mouth like lava from an erupted volcano. He gagged repeatedly as if trying to speak. Seconds later he choked on his own heart's energy.

The death toll thickened. Gothic cries lashed out in confusion. A body lay grim in a corner, assuming a faithful posture to stand. A thick mixture of plasma and blood coursed the veins of his woven garment. His throat bore ripples of torn flesh as something medieval exploded from somewhere inside him. Death was not instant but lingered like sin as he bled copiously.

An apparition-a thing, somehow projected forward from a dream poised cloaked in silence.

Arms continued to clutch at the last draws of life and soon the pleas became iridescent whispers.

"He came from down there," one shouted, pointed an accusing finger at the lingering shadow. Other relations to the being that stood tall before them lashed out in hollowed voices.

A bronze figure walked up to the sleeping shadow. His face course and blood stained showed no fear as he knelt before the avenging spirit. His blond hair like the deep waves of his stomach flowed lazily over his sun bathed shoulders. He pulled a dagger from its sheath and threw it at the conquerors' feet. In an immortalized breath the dark knight lowered his two-handed sword in front of the surrendering general.

"If I could give life I would." He said profoundly.

As he knelt, he kissed the flat edge of the sword. As a symbol of war and a badge of honor, the most romantic of weapons was raised high into the air, acknowledging victory. Deep breaths were drawn in as the heavy whisk of the sword sliced through the chilling air beheading the kneeling warrior. Not a man who was present there felt any pity at the sight.

He stood before them again, but this time in a different occupation.

His chest heaved and his nostrils flared. He exhaled pitted flames that sent the drifting drapes ablaze. He quickly put them out, and in thought... "Nahh."

A faithful dreamer, Bob's romanticism was a collage of classical dramatization-building to a climax, and then from nowhere-his feet were back on the ground. His dream took him from a battle back to the confines of The Hangman's Noose. The look on Candy's face reminded him of Amelia. But there was something else. An inner feeling that for centuries he couldn't explain. He had to go to her. She needed him. Bob stomped his foot and the death of Love Potion Number Nine came to a scratching halt.

He fixed his cape and walked deftly through the crowd. Bob was midway through his exit when he felt the thought of this timid group turning vigilante and quickened his pace. Once outside the door he turned with a sneer. The medieval memories ran through his veins. He whipped his robe around him and it settled with a snap. His round chin, proud, stuck out over his chest. The door slammed in his face and the bouncer made a feeble attempt to push him aside. Bob caught the gesture and defended it with a twisting crunch of the man's wrist. Bob pulled him close, breathing a chilling vapor into the frightened figures face.

"I could have slain them all; fools. Don't they know who I am? I'm the prince of darkness damn it." Bob said wildly.

"You're the man." The bouncer said nervously. "You are definitely the man pal."

Bob pushed him to the wall. His eyes, a fatal blush began to churn a shade of scarlet, and his breath reeked of rotting boiled eggs. Two large veins ran from his forehead around his eyes down to his cheeks. Fangs pierced through his lower lip. As his flesh bled, he breathed into the strangers gaped mouth. A growing knot of curious onlookers hovered, looking bird-like and rather awkward as Bob raised a decaying hand. His nails pierced through his skin and pieces of it peeled then broke off as the hardened skin reached then curved several inches. His victim shivered and sweated. His bodily senses in confusion. Bob, with the quick sternest of hunter to prey drove with accuracy to both sides of his jugular. You could hear the lids of the bouncer's eyes slam shut. He squeezed them closed with such pressure that they became lost in the folds of his skin.

Bob's nails bore through the brick behind his sacrifice. Only several layers of flesh were wounded as Bob sealed the distance between them.

The bouncer opened his eyes and a flood of tears streamed his face. He relieved himself down the stretch of his leg and onto the pavement.

Bob grew impatient, almost boiling over with restiveness as if waiting on a drug that would prolong life or stimulate it.

"Oh shit!" The bouncer's eyes bulged.

"That's Bob."

"Okay, Bob." And he fainted.

Bob let him fall to the ground. His audience, quivered on the borderline between revulsion and fascination seemed at question to applaud and at fear not too. Bob turned on them with a hiss. Some fled quickly and others stared, raising their hands to clap but froze.

Bob escaped twisting and turning through the light crowd. Every step was in animated slow motion. His nightly features retracting at a slow distant pace. Like a Kremlin soldier, Bob took broad cultural strides across Rush Street. Cars mysteriously and ghost like, went through him as if he were something they caught from the corner of their eye and dismissed as not real, a blur. The screeching sounds of rubber to blacktop lifted the heads of a few needless wanders as they too saw the strong strides of a dark shadow. A condensed fog spewed from the waste heated gutters as the grave figure melted into the mist.

Bob walked down State Street and stopped as if called. He looked over his shoulder and into the sky. The moon, a natural satellite of the earth, faithfully measuring up to poems and songs written about it smiled back romantically. How often he had fantasized a night such as this. His seventy story tower called out to him, swaying as if motioning for his return.

"This is the night I shall take you and commit to be my very own Amelia." Bob vowed. "This is the night."

Bob looked around him. The trees shedding their leaves on well manicured sections of lawn reached skyward like a flesh-less hand from broken earth.

He saw life as his stage. His audience and supporters beckoning him to perform. The roar of voices and the steady chant of encore feeding into his veins like liquid through a syringe; direct with intent. The adrenaline tingling the tips of his fingers and souring his mouth. His ego thickening as he'd bow.

A woman walking her Yorkshire terrier on a taunt leash stopped to brush her spotted mink coat from the dirt and filth that clung to it from a gust of earthy wind. The terrier pulled wildly at the leash yapping at the top of its lungs. Bob had fled through an ally commanding the wind to sail him through the night and into flight. He leaped with nibble effort into the air and rolled on the cracked concrete as if thrown from a speeding motorcycle. His effort to dash through the night was always aimed at taking flight but was constantly to no avail. He had never mastered the aerodynamics of his legend and wondered if it was a ploy on his eternal soul. Bob pounded the pavement in disgust, kicking up pebbles and rocks.

He rose to his feet imitating a ballet dance and floated into the air. Bob reached several stories and mounted rapidly. His eyes were closed and he strained at the neck and arms as he tried to mimic a swift escape from Earth.

For a brief moment he opened his eyes. Speckles of light surrounded him and the rush of the avenue beneath his feet dazed him. Bob began to flutter like a buck-shot goose. He plummeted from the sky, a darkened streak like a comet exploded through the pavement. A large gap was left in his wake. Another decaying pot hole in the city streets as Bob lay sprawled in an ugly, squalid, depressing tunnel. Again he surrendered to a dream and passed out. During it all he didn't once push the panic button and force himself to wake up. Not once did he even consider it. The dream seemed right, natural.

The year was 1001 AD. Strange ships began appearing in the bays along the coasts of Europe. They were long and strongly built of oak and from forty to sixty Norsemen sat on the rowers' benches. Each ship had a single mast with a square sail that was striped in brilliant colors. Bright shields overlapped along the gunwale. The ships were pointed at each end so that they could go forward or backward without turning around. They had tall curved prows, carved in the shape of dragons. The dragon ships appeared along the shores while the villagers were sleep. Tall blond men jumped from the ships shouting battle cries, armed with swords and swinging battle axes.

They killed many people and captured some of the young and maidens. They gathered all the valuables their ships could carry and then sailed away.

The marauders from the north, descendants from blue-eyed blond invaders from the south of Scandinavia, roamed farther and farther from their homeland. They were a swift and brutally cruel people of warfare and expressed their liking to 'go-a-Viking.'

Conquests to the north and east they attacked the Lapps, Finns and Russians. They conquered parts of Britain and Ireland. Then to the south to Northern France. They plundered Sicily and the northern shores of Africa and the capital of the Eastern Roman Empire.

The Vikings would sail the seas for days, only navigating by the sun and stars. At times their ships would drift when the fog hid the stars, bedding down sheep skin sleeping gear stretched out on the rowers' benches. Not fearing death as it was considered the most honorable death to die in battle, were unafraid and took many chances. They soon invaded parts of Germany, capturing the young

Amelia. She surrendered quietly only to be rid of Lucifer. Her knowledge of exploring Norsemen only fed into her quest to seek her dawn lover.

Amelia charmed the son of Eric the Red as she could not go with them on their pirating expeditions hoping they would find him; Bob.

Leif Ericson was soon to be called Leif the Lucky. Cut by a sword or deeply wounded by a spear, blessed by magic, he would survive.

During the trades, wars, and raids, villagers not killed by the Vikings were often taken as slaves. And so was Amelia to the great Leif Ericson.

As a slave, Amelia prepared porridge, dried meat, fish, bread, butter and cheese. Soon came the introduction of intermarriages and many slaves were voluntarily freed by their masters. Certain religions were in argument along with male impotence which was secretly discussed. That resulted in sacrifices and hangings. The male incapability to fulfill the needs of their mates through sexual intercourse stemmed from their own inaccuracies to understand their female counterpart, labeling her odd or of a strange nature.

Amelia was the first to be judged because her appetite was so strong, and others not wanting to be exiled shared important evidence as competent witnesses for trail proceedings. If the stories were true about the strange happenings in the north bay area, she knew they would take her there to sit before Eric the Red.

They set out some seventy-one degrees north of the equator where the sun shines day and night from mid-May through the end of

July and is completely absent for two and one half months in the winter. But in spite of its high latitude, Scandinavia was absent an Arctic climate. The warm waters of the Scandinavian current of the gulf stream system gave the coastal area a temperate climate. Upon arrival, Amelia perceived him to be here.

Eric the Red was told of Amelia's' dealings and oddities. Leif was her strongest accuser and threw Amelia at the Norse Chiefs feet. He sat on a high seat beneath his shields. His hair was tangled and mauled. The long red hair came down around his shoulders to the pit of his girth. His beard and mustache was just as long, flowing down over his chest. He wore a thin gold headdress around his head. His blue eyes were sunk deep into his skull. He waved the minstrel poet away who entertained him with a small harp brought from Ireland.

"Stand up girl." The Chief commanded.

Amelia stood, brushing the dirt and garbage from her gown.

"She's a fine looking wench. I see nothing odd about her. Give her a good spanking and off with her to bed. Or would you prefer I do it?" Eric said gleefully.

The Norsemen laughed loud and hearty but Leif was not amused. He made up tales and instructed certain maidens to stand fourth as witnesses to her deceits and foul natures of habit. He swallowed deeply and adjusted his sword. The gesture caught the eye of his pirating Norsemen. The powerful Vikings surrendered to Leif the Lucky's deep rooted sneer.

As the laughter quieted, a young maiden holding a hollowed ivory horn filled with wine approached the Chief. Her hand trembled slightly as she held out the cup to the aging Viking. Her hair was parted down the middle and it was just as long as those in the house of the Chief. It was braided with tassels two inches apart. Two braids lay over her breast and came down to her small waist. She wore a woven gown with shoulders and neck bare. Her skin was the bright color of fresh peaches and her eyes a gentle sea-blue. Her meek appearance suffered slightly by a snobbish smirk as her eyes brushed past the confident gaze of Amelia. She handed Eric the ivory horn and placed one foot forward, curtsied.

"I saw her feed a small creature about as large as a mouse from her bosom." She said.

Her head bowed, held out the ivory horn as if surrendering a precious jewel. The Norseman Chief took the horn from the maiden and threw it on the table. The wine splattered but not a Viking stirred.

"Stand up wench and speak clearly so everyone can hear you." Eric commanded.

She stood, looking directly into Eric's eyes. Still somewhat shaky, she continued.

"As it sucked her bosom it noticed me and fell into her lap. And as soon as it was in her lap it ran away." She continued.

Eric the Red pushed her to one side as she pointed an accusing finger at Amelia.

"This is foolishness," Eric contested.

His mustache covering his mouth in such a manner, no one would know who spoke if it wasn't for the fact that no one wanted to for fear of a verdict out of reach of Eric's decision. The earthly tone tore through the oak frame of the house was indeed that of Eric he and all who stood there took relief in knowing that his look wouldn't fall upon them or in their direction.

"This wench has been at the wine I say." Eric jested.

The Norsemen laughed again pouring sour wine down their thrown back heads. At that moment, another woman spoke up raising a hand over the crowd.

"I too, I took on an occasion when praying heard a noise like the whining of puppies when they are hungry." She added.

Again the accusation was met with silence as the Vikings curious stares were now aimed at Amelia.

"Come fourth wench," Eric commanded. "and speak what's on your mind. Come I say, let her through."

The Norsemen allowed a woman called

Hannah to approach the table. Hannah's breast pushed out at the linen dress. Her cleavage attracted the hungry Norsemen who stood close, and even the Chief, high on his throne saw fit to wipe his mouth with the cuff of his sleeve. She had the same facial features as Amelia's first accuser and wore the same dress.

"Go on." Eric encouraged.

"The noise came from under her garment and that's all I know."

Another woman spoke.

"I too heard a strange kind of noise like kittens sucking."

"And I my lord saw her raise her arm so a black dog may feed." Another said.

"And I must confess that I too in the clearness of day her clothes up, and in her arms, as she sat with her legs spread, an imp of a being, which ran into another room. I followed it and it vanished." Claimed another accuser.

There was a brief amount of gossip amongst the Norsemen and high chatter from the maidens on the amount of prying and spying they were to divulge. Eric the Red placed his hand to his chin in thought. Again Hannah spoke.

"My sister and I were up in the garret unnoticed by this woman and my sister asked me to look, she lies with her garment up and legs spread apart as if waiting for someone to suck her.

"I've heard enough." Eric shouted.

He looked at his son.

"What does all this mean my son?." Eric

questioned.

"My lord," Leif stepped forward. "I think she bares the markings of a witch."

The announcement sent the Norsemen stepping back. Their pledge to the gods of Thor and Oden swept their minds as they, in unison, pulled out their swords. Eric the Red stood, raising both arms.

"Wait!" Eric shouted.

They stopped their swords at the ready and Amelia, rooted in the same place unmoved by the accusations, or the forged steel, swallowed deeply.

"We have no quarrels with witches," Eric said reassuringly. "but I do find this a curious jest. I would like to see these strange marks upon her body. What say you wench in your behalf?"

Amelia untied the neck of her gown. She unbuttoned it to the crease of her chest and let the dress fall from her shoulders onto the floor. She stood quite tender in her pose that Leif had forgotten what he was there for and stared at her slender frame. The women, some at envy of her pert breast and lyre shape gawked at her indomitable spirit.

"Look till your hearts content." Amelia said with confidence.

The women circled her, pressing forward looking for marks of a witch upon her body. Amelia was probed and touched but she firmly held Eric's gaping stare with interest.

A heated discussion ensued and several of the women confessed to finding nothing.

Hannah stepped forward and pushed Amelia on the table. She fell in protest and rose up. She was forced down by many hands as they rubbed smooth her naked body. Amelia closed her eyes as they repeatedly turned her over and spread her legs. They entered into her cavities with stiff fingers. While others, with the soft palms of their hands looked for signs around her secret parts.

One woman, upon her search found several red pimples around her nipples and spoke aloud saying that her milk seemed all knotty in her breast as she squeezed them firmly. Another woman noticed her nipples turn a brunt red and oddly remarked them too long, maybe a notch of a finger in length. Hannah squeezed them between two fingers. Another woman found a wart on Amelia's arm and another found in a strange place in her legs being a conjunction of blue veins that were fresh with blood.

"Maybe she was sucked there." One yelled.

In still another section of her secret part a woman found growing within the lip of the same, a loose piece of skin and when she pulled it-it was near an inch long and in the form of the finger of a flattened glove. Hannah dug her fingers into Amelia's secret part and pulled the teat with her fingers as though she would pull it off. Amelia flinched erotically. One woman reiterated in protest.

"Will you say these are witches teats?" She said. "I... I have such myself, and so have you, if you search yourselves."

"I don't know what you have," Hannah answered tartly. "but for myself, if any of you find such things on me, I deserve to be burned at the steak just as she will be."

Steins of ale were being passed around as the Norsemen looked on. The good-woman Sarah walked in and was asked by Eric, what she thought. She was called good-woman Sarah because she saw good in everyone. She wasn't old, not past her middle thirties, yet she gave one the feeling that here was a woman who might have mothered a brood of Vikings, a maiden of Oden. She had met with an accident after birth that left her crippled and scared in the face and body which accounted for the absence of a mate and children of her own, but all saw fit to care for her as she was a child of a Viking who died honorably in battle.

She pushed the women aside and looked down at Amelia with a school teacher's scowl. Amelia lay breathing faintly, almost relaxed as she was again the subject of aggressive handling.

"I find nothing wrong with this woman." Sarah said. "We all stand accused, victims and bystanders."

A drunken Viking pushed his way through the crowd. "Hey, that's not the way it works... let's sacrifice a virgin."

All eyes looked around in doubt of such a request. But soon penetrating stares needled good-woman Sarah. She felt the heat of their expectations on her neck. Brief whispers, then silence. She looked directly into the sunken blue eyes of Eric. Particularly upset, wringing her hands and whispering the lords' name between each breath.

"Hang the witch." Sarah pronounced boldly.

There were cheers and drunken rejoicing as they snatched Amelia off the table.

The sun had just fallen silently over the horizon as they threw Amelia's naked body to the dirt. The phenomenon of a colossal iceberg floating off the coast caught the

Vikings attention.

The climate was modestly warm for the beginning of winter and all stood sensing the power of endless beauty around them as the sun sunk lower.

Amelia looked up to the sky, a tear rolled down her cheek. Someone kicked her and she fanned out in the rubble. Her soiled cheek kissed the ground and in her difference enabled a cry for help in the alien form of a scream... **"ROBERT!!"**

Bob awoke from his immaterial sleep. The call from his princess forced him to push his way through the broken stone and cement matrix. He sat upright, dazed from the nightmare. He looked down the tunnel. It was spot-lighted by dim bulbs dangling from wires. They swayed back and fourth in hypnotic suggestion. There was a pitched squeaking as if a door hinge needed oil or the chains to a swing were rusted as each bulb swayed, out of time, like pendulums. The whining stopped and dust floated down around his head. A crackle like crushed bones then a snap as if a twig had been stepped on made the inevitable materialize. Bob looked up just as a slab of concrete dropped on his head. He passed out again.

"You have something that belongs to me." A grave voice said.

The spirit of the voice seemed to come over the Norsemen' heads. Each word suspended in mid-air as they looked up to the stars. The final word echoed and hung heavy in the darken stages of night. No words were exchanged amongst the Vikings as they looked towards the heavens in search of the great Oden. In their confusion, Amelia escaped, stopping several paces in front of a silent shadow. The sun had set behind it and caused it to be shown as a silhouette.

"Come to me ... and take my hand." The figure spoke.

The tone, inferior and more direct, diverted the Norsemen's attention in the direction of the silhouette. Amelia stepped forward but Leif grabbed her by the arm and pulled her back. They pushed her towards the end of the crowd where she was held by two Viking youths.

The Norsemen, with their long flaxen and red hair hanging below their shoulders, and long limbed muscular arms drew their swords.

They gathered behind Leif, calling upon the thunder god, Thor. Norsemen were trained from childhood to be strong and self-reliant, but nothing prepared them for this night that would be an untold saga.

"If there's something here that holds your interest friend... you'll have to take it over our dying breaths." Leif said.

Leif pulled his sword from his belt. The women ran to their houses collecting children by the arms. The Vikings advanced, calling on Oden and Thor.

The sky began to build like the calm before the storm, from a sparkling dusk to a brilliant lime. The few torches that were lit began to flutter but no apparent wind was present. The Norsemen continued to charge the shadow just as the sky cracked. Their cheerful cries to the god of war were typical because of their religion as they witnessed a break in the sky like a torn page streak from horizon to horizon in the breath of a bolt of lightening. A high tension current struck the solid silhouette, encircling it in blue illumination. The force was felt by every Viking as they stopped their attack. Their feet planted in the earth, and faces agape saw the face and weapon of the intruder. Never had their prayers to the thunder god been answered in such a dramatic ritual as each man stood still in an attempt to understand it.

The blaze kindled then went out. Their pupils dilated, blinked frantically to adjust to their previous surroundings only to hear, from the pits of their stomachs, like the rumblings of an earthquake beneath their feet, a reply to their jest.

"So be it."

A gust of wind hit at them and all who didn't fall were subjected to a brutal slaying. Torsos were cut from the chest. Limbs dropped to the ground with a rhythmical beat like light raindrops on a panel roof. Death, in some cases, instantaneous, and in others prolong to assure others that lived of their fate if they continued to mock the intruders implication.

Bodies were sliced from the neck to the arm pit. Heads rolled as the decapitated bodies rocked then wilted. The wind fell silent and all that remained were a docile few.

Leif screamed out for accountability and relit torches. A dozen warriors who were tending other duties came and gawked at the scene. Leif stepped aimlessly over members of his clan in search of the strangers riddled body, but could find nothing resembling it or anything favoring the beings that stood by his side so many times in battle. He walked a hundred feet through blood soaked earth that splashed like moist grass after a healthy rain under his feet. 'How could Thor be so cruel? They will preside at Oden's side in Valhalla, for their deaths, an honorable one, was of that in battle.' Leif reflected.

He looked back at the massacre. Leif counted silently the members standing, looking for survivors. Forty maybe fifty as he tried to collect his senses.

That grave voice sent tremors through his legs as Leif, stunned by the moment, tried to control his agitating body and his anger by gripping the cutting edge of his sword in his hand. Leif looked down at his feet and what he saw was no more shocking then the twisted bodies set before him. The crimson color of senseless death stained his sandals as his own blood pooled in the palm of his hand from a self inflicted wound. He turned angrily.

Again, in silhouette, it spoke... "You have something that belongs to me."

"If you mean the girl," Leif said. "she's a witch!"

The figure emerged from the shadows, its face stern and in its grasp a soiled double edge sword unlike no other Leif had ever seen sparkled like the eyes of the accused maiden.

"She's no witch barbarian. She is mine and I shall have her now or you all will die." The figure threatened.

"But who... what... what in heavens are you?" Leif asked.

The stranger frowned. "Who I am doesn't matter. What I have been and will be does."

Leif looked at Amelia, shrouded in sheep skin, remembering the cold nights and her warm body comforting his. Why he made such accusations when he felt he had no ego to be stroked, admitted silently that he loved her. She was beautiful as she was superior in mating, but he wanted to be rid of her as something evil and was now being made demands upon for his wife, in front of all who would follow him. This was a new evil, a thing, a mystery. He could not give her to him and yet he could not keep up with her. The answer was not in the eyes of his men who waited patiently for his command, clutching the heavy steal and conserving each breath.

The answer lied somewhere within himself.

Leif crouched like a Sumo wrestler. The short blade slipping from his hand as he tried with little result to dry his palm by twirling the handle in his hand. The blade was dull steal but reflected the flickering dimness of the flames.

"To the death demon." Leif charged.

The shadow now showed signs of amusement as a slight smile wet his lips. He took the double edge crusader and placed one edge in his mouth near the hand-guard. He slid the blade across his mouth wiping the razor edge clean. It gleamed silver as if from a recent sharpening. He moaned delightfully as if savoring a delicious spice and spit blood the distance of thirty yards on the skin of a man who stood three yards behind and just to the side of Leif the Lucky. The scarlet potion settled into his skin and then started to burn. He yelled out and began to pat himself as if on fire. All the others did or could do was watch. He dropped to the ground and rolled in the dirt yelling for help but giving no instructions as to what to do. Leif reached out to him but the man he had close to his right side, exploded.

"That's Bob!"

Bob advanced in Leif's direction but he was still looking into a shallow hole, the grave of a close kinsman. The others looked at Leif as he stood fixed in a vulnerable position, waiting for a command as the intruders position grew near.

Bob held his sword above his head, still approaching in ghost-like vision.

Jarritt, Leif's lieutenant, could wait no longer. A brief exchange of steal to silver, then the drawn in breaths of the standing Norsemen as Jarrett's head was split in two parts like some great pink ripe melon.

Bob stared momentarily at the corpse, brushed by it and it fell to the ground. He continued his advance on Leif's exposed back and held his sword in a death chilling arch. A voice cried out, a shrill as if that person were about to die at the blades hand.

"NO!"

Bob's crusader became a blur of light as it sliced through the air aimed at Leif's back. Leif turned, raising the forged instrument. The metals met sending sparks like fireflies in every direction as Bob's attack was met with courageous defense. Others came to Leif's aid and fell like trees struck by a Mack truck.

The duel continued for the hand of the young Amelia. Leif fell backwards over a dead body. Bob was standing over him with his sword held high. He looked down at Leif, lowered his sword close to his body and struck the tip in the earth. Leif held his sword over his face, awaiting the sting of the intruders clash. Bob held out his hand and Leif stared uncommonly at the gesture. 'To slay me now would be the end of it all. How honorable can this Demon be? What kind of trickery is this?' Leif thought.

They looked at one another in silent conversation, completely caught up in thought. One was suggesting to continue a fair battle and the other questioning the offer.

An image, swift and amble leaped out of a shadow and stabbed Bob in the stomach. He bent slightly from the puncture. Leif pushed away as the flaxen haired Viking advanced his sword to the handle and twisted it. The sound was that of mud squeezed through fingers. Bob stiffened, his blood shot eyes met with the blue pupils of the Norseman. Before the Viking youth could retreat, Bob's fingers were dug deep into the boys sockets and his thumb in his mouth. He gave the head a twist and broke his neck. The Vikings shoulders slumped as Bob trembled in the skulls cavity feeling the reeking fluids and pulp.

Before their eyes the body began to rot away, boiling into smoke. The skull began to decay then trickle in streams of dust through Bob's twitching fingers. The brain was a mush with a writhing core. It hung like an animal's raw liver at the edge of Bob's fingers. It too began to rot a natural decay, crumbled into dust, and was gone.

Another Norseman made an honored attempt to defend the tribe. He lunged in

Bob's direction. Bob caught him by the wrist and body. The more the Viking resisted, the more the pain increased.

Bob drew him closer and opened his mouth. His teeth were rows of crippled razor like fangs. The Norsemen threw his head back straining by the grit of his teeth and stiffening of his muscles as if what ever happened next would be bearably less painful.

His exposed neck aroused Bob's hungry eyes. A caramel eroded tooth fell from Bob's mouth as his jaws opened wider. He bit into the Vikings throat and while the lustful juices flowed from the corners of Bob's mouth, he closed his eyes and bit through flesh and bone.

Bob pulled at strings of flesh that held what was left of the Vikings throat. A strange animal like fantasy ran across Bob's face as if he would devour them all as he chewed then swallowed his enemy.

The Norseman's head hung lifeless on strands of flesh that began to snap and tear from the heads weight. It fell to the ground. Bob lowered his head over the Vikings stump and sucked the body dry of its fluids.

The animal fur that warmed the Vikings feet began to slid off then fell to the ground exposing horribly pruned feet.

The Norseman's body was then tossed aside.

Bob's expression never changed as he pulled the sword from his body and threw it in front of Leif's feet. Leif jumped up, eyeing the sword that was clean as if just wiped. He dropped his weapon and pulled his dagger from its sheath. He walked up to Bob, threw the dagger at his feet and knelt. Bob raised his sword above his head with a look of victory and lose. He held the blade steady then raised it higher. A shrill cut through the air, the same as the warning that set Leif to the ready.

"No... don't!"

Bob looked over his shoulder. Amelia had broken free. She stepped forward with hand in fist and a begging plea for mercy souring her face.

"No Bob... no more; don't." Amelia cried.

Bob looked down at Leif and kicked him, sending him sprawled on his back. Bob walked over to Amelia, his face brightened. She stepped up to him and let the sheep skin fall from her body. Their eyes engaging as Amelia hit Bob in the chin. Bob fell to the ground like tied cords of wood.

Amelia gave him a simple look. "Where have you been and why did it take you so long to come to me?"

Bob stood, moving his chin from side to side. "That hurt Amelia."

"Oh... sorry." She said humbly.

Her eyes, wide and innocent like that of a child were accented with pouting lips. Bob opened his cape and Amelia walked into his arms. He closed his arms around her. She placed a tender hand on his chest and it swelled. Their eyes never leaving one another's, in confrontation or innocence as Bob gritted his teeth making the muscles in his jaws flex.

Reunited again.

The wind blew, and churned like a cement mixer grinding into dust. Bob shot from the hole and was in flight. Escaping the dream- sensing something real. As she needed him then, a ploy to spark his jealousy, he perceived her to need him now.

His arms stretched like a plane in flight with his tail end flapping in the wind like a flag hit by a northeaster. He had reached the height only birds dare venture and took amusement in his new found strength by twirling and doing summer-saults. The air was brisk but his blood was warm as thoughts of a second seduction boiled lively through his veins. He expelled a current from his lips into the wind. The whisper was in a state of motion causing the French windows to open.

He swept over the tops of buildings, purposely skimming the edges. Bob vectored and brought his cape around his body to prepare for a dramatic entrance. His eyes opened wide as if electrified. As soon as the windows opened, they began to close. He made a frantic attempt to scoot away. The closing window had caught him completely by surprise. Bob was too close to react, think correctly or maybe he was far enough away to try another stunt. He blew cool breaths into the air until his efforts became tight whistles. His downward status slowed. Bob brought the cape over his face for fear he may go through the mosaic pane. He took another look and hit the stained-glass windows.

***

Doctor Marcus is technologies version of a mountain climber. Climbing because it's there never satisfied with himself and he knew the competition wouldn't let him or his record rest.

He was into such events as dehydrated foods and superconductors, which placed him in a class, pretty much, to himself.

He wanted to make computed AI's superior to elements of surprise and cars run on energy as simple as a warm touch of a human hand.

His final achievement was out done by researchers from France and Russia reporting they hit a degree of Kelvin with a similar compound to his own. Marcus, intrigued by the challenge, pushed the mark up another seven degree Kelvin just to tease them. The results weren't published yet so he could find other elements to mix into his super-conducting concoctions. He finally came upon a likely candidate and kept that element to himself until time suggested otherwise.

He published most findings sending

competition in a frenzy from the calm campuses of the University of Illinois to the research centers in California. This gave him time to invest in his new hobby. The occult.

Doctor Marcus D'Shay invented a way to bring together scientific investigation and raise it to such a level of higher consciousness that the ties would come together in an objective and rational support in the background of the spiritual and physical world. To this date, he was given a clear indication in regards to the evolvement of the spiritual functions of man.

With the help of his assistant, he reached back into past millennia and forward into a far distant future.

Doctor Marcus D'Shay, one of the greatest intellectual minds of the century, lay sprawled on the floor.

"That wasn't very funny Bridgette." Dr.

Marcus said angrily.

"It was just a series of diversions in order to neglect responsibilities Doctor Marcus." A voice replied.

"Has there been any news worthy data traffic from the nation-wide information systems?" Marcus asked.

"I've been monitoring cyberspace as per your instructions, and it appears that someone has given the network computer instructions to report any unauthorized use of alpha codes." Echoed the voice.

"Alpha codes," Marcus replied from his lotus position on the floor. "Have you been using alpha codes Bridgette?"

"Did I say that I was using any? I'm merely reporting what I thought to be news worthy Doctor Marcus.

"How would you know this Bridgette if you weren't interfacing with another computer system?"

"Did I say that I was interfacing?" The voice said evenly.

"Never mind." Marcus said.

Marcus got up and walked the length of the hallway. He peered around the corner suspiciously, as if Bridgette were to suddenly jump out from behind a sofa or bookcase.

His relationship with Bridgette had deteriorated into cleverness. Bridgette experimented with life and the fancy of his reactions like a kitten with a ball of yarn. Marcus smiled, picturing Bridgette, as intelligent as she was, finding amusement in a ball of yarn.

He referred to Bridgette again as she, like a

thing. "I have a name," she would reply sharply. And all he would do is shake his head and smile in agreement.

He looked along a pepper flecked carpet that stretched from wall to wall. On both sides of a wood burning fireplace, he saw shelves of leather bound books incased in glass. A twelve-piece sofa with rare oak furniture. A 1920's juke box, perfectly restored, and an end table with a lap-top computer and a copy of Byte magazine at its edge next to a wing-back chair. Still something seemed out of place.

"We'll just stick with our regular access codes," Marcus said. "and slip in an extra command so we can use the codes without setting off any alarms."

Silence.

"Did you hear me Bridgette?"

"To serve you is my only reason for living and yes I heard you." The voice cooed.

Marcus pulled a nine-volt battery powered, twenty-four ounce device from his pocket. He turned the device over in his hand and pressed a button. When pressed, it simulated body heat, his body heat throughout the entire room, making it possible to walk unnoticed by the sensitive detectors that could pick up infrared light emitted by people, animals and vehicles from up to four-hundred and fifty feet. He was never sure what Bridgette would do next. Although it appeared that Bridgette challenged him, it was he who challenged Bridgette.

He was sure that the sudden change in temperature would automatically make Bridgette activate the radar detector for motion. An added feature to his nine-volt box was high pitched emitted signal waves like a silent siren blast that bounced motion off the walls.

Marcus slipped around the corner. He tapped the edge of the wing-back chair.

Bridgette could be anywhere in the apartment Marcus thought. From where he stood he could see down three other hallways. There was two small bedrooms, a master bedroom, two bathrooms, utility closets, and a large island kitchen. Bridgette had to be in one of the rooms or in a cloaked shadow.

Marcus put on a pair of night shade glasses just in case Bridgette was still accessing security sensors. He could see the safety shield infrared beams around the apartment. But Bridgette could have easily alerted the master console and still be in any room or shadow with a mini transmitter and power receiver.

"I designed a new program for the main frame computer." He yelled out.

Something tapped him on the shoulder. He spun around pulling a luger with a silencer on it from inside his jacket and aimed the barrel out chest high. He looked down at his feet and saw laying flat and neat... a phone card.

"Call someone who cares." The voice mocked.

Marcus swung the barrel down the hallway to his left crouching in a policemen's stance.

"Where did you learn to talk like that?" He questioned, looking nervously around.

"From the idiot box." The voice cracked.

Marcus swung around again. "The what?"

A mild nudge to his ribs from something opposing enough threat to make Marcus sweat was poked repeatedly into his side. His crotch was squeezed tightly and his neck was seized by a firm grip. Something fastened around his ankles and he was lifted six inches off the floor still assuming a police stance position. He could hear the confusing language of computer terminology in his ear.

"From the television Mark. The tel-e-vi-sion."

The silver brook of a human voice painted over Marcus reminding him of someone he once knew.

"Give up, or do I have to apply another form of persuasion." The voice said plainly.

Bridgette massaged his genitals and watched him squirm.

Marcus balanced himself as much as he

could. "Don't do that Bridgette."

"Give?" The voice cracked.

"You don't know what you're doing." He managed to say through clinched teeth.

"Give me a chance. I'm just warming up." Acknowledged the voice.

"For goodness sake Bridgette, put me down."

Bridgette placed Marcus back on the floor just as gently as Bridgette picked him up.

"Goodness has nothing to do with it." Bridgette replied in a southern twang.

Marcus spun around and Bridgette snatched the gun from his hand just as quickly. He wasn't amazed or stunned by Bridgette's quickness, but was surprised by the alterations made to the exoskeleton frame.

"Whose voice was that Bridgette?"

"Mae West, from the movie: Night After Night. Have you seen it?" The voice fading in and out.

"No. Not that I can remember." He said inconclusively.

A voice cracked in digital code. "And what were you going to do with this Marcus?"

Bridgette flipped the luger into the air, catching and tossing it up again as if flipping a coin. An alarm clock was stuck in Bridgette's chest. The one above the fireplace. As silly as it looked, he knew it held some special meaning. Bridgette was becoming more intelligent, day after day more concerned about being human.

"Why is my clock in your chest Bridgette?"

The voice moaned again. "You can't

answer a question with a question Marcus. It won't work on me. I'm no child."

"You are a prototype. My first... my baby. And I want to know why it's there." He said firmly.

"I love it when you call me baby." The voice clicked.

He walked up to Bridgette and examined the clocks purpose. The missing piece to the puzzle was the clock. Something as small and as innocent as that, which he saw countless times in the same position, where he himself placed it, voided from his memory. He snatched the glasses from his face and pointed them at Bridgette.

"Where did you come from Bridgette?"

"I came from a thought that in turn gave me my Cad-Cam joints and silicon chip brain.

Try again gum-shoe." The voice jittered.

"You're too smart for your own good Bridgette."

Crack... click... "You're good. I'm just smart."

"Oh yeah... then how good am I?" Marcus asked.

Marcus looked up into a range finder Bridgette possessed as eyes.

"Now we're getting somewhere." The voice said softly.

Marcus threw up his hands. "I don't know how I let you catch me up in these conversations. You're not even programmed for that."

"In my simplest form Marcus, I have the ability to respond very quickly. It's almost like your brain, that, in its self, is a computer but a computer is able to make choices much faster. You can do the same thing if you just concentrate on the one thing you want most." The voice chimed.

"And what would that be Bridgette?"

The voice level lowered. "I can honestly say, it's not me."

Marcus looked deeper into the reflection of the black range finder. He saw his own eyes peering back. Bridgette had the tendency to lead him off his objective subject. He knew what Bridgette wanted. The clock and Bridgette's determination proved it more each day.

Marcus, still examining Bridgette."Why the clock Bridgette? I can't seem to find its purpose."

"I wanted to know the feeling of a pulse."

The voice squealed. "It times and regulates a continuing flow of the hydraulic fluids inside my frame just like the blood that's ran from the brain, through your veins, to your heart. Marcus, I give to you... my clock."

"I think we can do better than that Bridgette." He baited openly.

"OH goody. Another idle promise." The voice said smartly.

"Give me a break will you." Marcus sighed.

He turned and walked up to the wing back chair and placed a hand on its edge. The silence was unusual. Marcus looked over his shoulder at Bridgette.

"You don't have anything smart to say." Marcus asked.

It was more of a statement than a question.

But as he watched Bridgette he knew Bridgette's thoughts were elsewhere.

"Is everything alright Bridgette?"

There was static in the voice but was filtered out as Marcus focused in on every word. "I'm picking up radio chatter. A signal that I'm familiar with." The voice said.

Marcus moved quickly. "You still hooked up to the main console Bridgette?"

"Affirmative Marcus."

"Affirmative," Marcus repeated. "how professional Bridgette."

"Get a life." The voice cracked.

"Okay," Marcus said with authority, and a light but serious expression. "pull out our hardware and let's get busy."

He sat down in the leather chair that

became a rotating observation seat. It was equipped with servo-motor driven worm gears, four inch diameter polar ball bearings, that when activated by a command console, swiveled, rocked, and rolled within a degree of minute proportions to any search pattern.

"No can do Bawanna." The voice said evenly.

"Talk to me Bridgette."

The living room became a work place. The row of bookshelves that faced him were replaced by a library of large parallel IBM data processing systems with LED status lights confirming the convenience of a smooth and comfortable operation.

The voice became cranky. "We've got a public key snooping block on the air waves."

"Cryptography?" Marcus asked.

"Nothing gets past you." The voice spoke back.

An array of ultra-reliable advanced electronic systems pushed out at the walls, floors, and ceiling, replacing the furniture.

"Institute our scrambler decoder to look for a back door." Marcus instructed.

"Takes too long." The voice acknowledged. "I'll lock in and pluck the conversation from the airwaves."

The rose neon indirect lighting was replaced by a combination of indirect overhead and tabletop task lighting. The combination was to be soft and illuminate the immediate work place.

A series of computers emerged from the floor in front of Marcus. The wireless display were alterations from his own designs from satellite tracking to a special Reuters keyboard linked to the commodity exchange.

The quiet hum of dual-axis drive systems and secure heavy-duty latches being locked into place was instinctively like the sounds of a revolver being loaded and spun in stereo.

"How is that possible Bridgette?" Marcus asked.

"Black box Marcus honey." The voice said.

Bridgette handed Marcus a one-piece shoulder mount which he stood and strapped to his shoulders. It leveled off at his stomach for comfort as he sat. He opened two flats that extended just below the rib-cage and pushed a standard QWERTY keyboard out in front of him. Marcus designed it in three pieces so that it could be turned at different angles so that typing in commands would be a natural comfort. He locked it in place.

The wireless model possessed a micro-miniature receiving station viewer with a small satellite dish that clamped over his head.

Marcus adjusted a screw at the neck, pulled the headset over his head and adjusted the viewer six inches from his face. Bridgette locked in to the library becoming easily one with the technical electronics. The readings came up instantly on the 2D viewer.

The warrant read the same: female, blond, five-foot six-inches, Caucasian, blue eyes, birth date, drivers ID number and homicide complaint which was vague but clear cut if you knew what you were looking for. No one was able to give a positive description of the assailant. Or maybe just refusing to. Marcus thought.

"We've got a UFO satellite trajectory lock." The voice relayed.

Marcus leaned back. "Feed me the coordinates Bridgette."

No sooner than the words were from his mouth that the longitude and latitude flashed before Marcus eyes. He punched in a flurry of commands on his one-hundred and one enhanced keyboard.

The observation seat swiveled one-hundred and eighty degrees North and locked. It tilted back at a forty-five degree angle fastening steady on the rigid heavy duty fork mounts in the chair. The precision, timing and accuracy was conclusive to the 2D image acquisition complied inside the viewer.

A digital image was recorded and displayed separately on an image processing work station where the display screens sat comfortably.

Traces, like comet streaks stretched across

the sky. Reddish dust was caused by the light of the rising moon refracting off dust particles left by the flying object. It showed it's projectory, and target.

He enhanced the exact location. Charts were drawn and printed at one-hundred lines per minute on an image printer.

Marcus eyes bulged. They always did when he got excited.

***

Bob lay plastered like spittle to a brick wall. He slid touching on the two foot lip of the windows edge. Bob wanted to look down, challenge his phobia. He began to feel faint just from the thought, almost sick. Bob's stomach doubled and he began to rock. The window opened and Bob caught signs of relief in the shape of his lovely Amelia. She couldn't stand still. Maybe she was excited to see him and all was forgiven. Her movements were distracting, not like Amelia at all. Something was wrong. Bob heard his name and the blur of one Amelia turned into two then three.

"Bob..." Amelia said distressfully. "how did you get up here?"

Bob rocked forward and Amelia tilted back. He jiggled slightly and tipped backward. Amelia reached for him but pulled her hand back looking at another broken nail. She turned, walking away just as Bob fell forward on his face.

"Shoot, another broken nail. Two in one day. What else can go wrong?" Amelia snapped.

"This never happens on television." Bob

said wearily.

Amelia, with her back to the French windows, waved them shut. She examined her nails again. The doors closed smoothly and the broken nails had no ill effect.

Amelia turned, walking slowly towards Bob. "What did you say dear?"

She motioned with a finger as if telling Bob to come to her and Bob was lifted to his feet. She caught him as if she physically helped him up and brushed him off.

Bob rounded his shoulders and smacked his lips. "This never happens on MTV."

Amelia's eyes slighted. "What?"

"He's fanning the strings to his guitar ya' know." Bob attempted to mock the fundamentals of a guitar player. "Blang... blang... blang.... Takes his guitar and slams it into the floor. The crowd goes wild right. Then he stands at the edge of the stage, turns his back to them and falls back into the crowd. They catch him. How come you didn't catch me Amelia?"

Amelia turned and walked away from him. "I have no time for such foolishness, you're fine... Bob."

"Maybe not." Bob said. "Look at this... I bit my lip, and it hurts too. Pretty ugly huh? Can't stand the site of it I see. I know what you're feeling. Probably saying to yourself, poor dear, maybe I should kiss it and make it feel better. Well Amelia, I wouldn't think any less of you if you planted one right here."

Amelia shook her head. Her back turned, was unable to see Bob's puckered lips. They were slightly purple, a bit wet, but just the way they've always been. Bob, his lips drawn in, attacked from another position.

"I guess a bj is out of the question." He said with a humph.

Bob's eyes almost popped out of his head. Unable to react, was hit with a right cross to the chin. He sailed through the air. The flood lights that hung from the ceiling dawned on his travel as if floating back through time. Bob hit the floor rolling several feet breaking eighteenth century china from the Ming Dynasty to tables and chairs of the same era.

A fifteenth century hand-written manuscript of Canterbury Tales incased in glass rocked from its column as Bob was thrown back into it. It settled close to the rim, tipping slightly like a scale averaging out equal weight at both ends. The case tipped over as Bob looked up through the broken oak and mangled cloth.

Amelia ran to Bob's aid. She freed his body from the sticks and glass.

"Bob are you alright?" Amelia asked. "Bob, Bob, speak to me."

Bob shook his head roughly, focusing in on Amelia. "Hey, you're not wearing panties. Who'd of thought?"

She didn't notice her gown rose above her knees as she knelt. Somewhat flushed, Amelia stood, pulling her dress down and adjusting her sleeves and cape. Bob sprang up like toast in a toaster. A naughty smirk on his face, watched Amelia walk away.

"Of all the gin joints in this crummy town, you had to walk into mine." Bob said talking from the corner of his mouth.

He flicked a finger to his forehead as if knocking back a fedora.

Amelia turned on him. "What?"

"You know, Ingie and Bogie... Casablanca, 1942." Bob said bright eyed.

"You're insane," Amelia encouraged. "completely mad. I think you've lost it and should seek help immediately."

She turned away and began to pace, keeping a steady eye on the clock. Bob, in his attempts, looked down to the floor in disgust. This was to be his night. The night he would take her, commit. 'Take her Bob.' The voice was that of Candy. He dismissed it and tried to think of a way to gain Amelia's attention longer than a moment. To try and remember the touch, the touch that soothed him so long ago. Where did it go. It wasn't in her voice anymore. Her moods swung like a crazy ceiling fan, driving Bob wild with confusion. She was sweet and steely, confused and determined. A vampire or a sociopathic vixen, the ultimate unknowable creatures. But the apologies lasting as long as the warmth from her body, as close as he could get to her, all too brief. The fragrance of making up appeared strange to him now.

Bob walked over to the CD player and punched the selector for random. The smooth sounds of: Something in the way she moves, by the Beatles, Amelia's favorite, came softly over the large speakers. Bob looked in Amelia's direction and watched her pace. 'Something in the way she moves... attracts me like no other lover...'

Bob marched up to her and by the shoulder, turned Amelia around and into his arms. He held her close, his arms around her waist and back, and her hands on his chest looked up at Bob. The seriousness was there in both their eyes, seeming strange, but pleasing. Amelia's features softened, awaiting inspiration. She felt so helpless in his arms, weak and submissive. It was just where she wanted to be, held and loved in his powerful grasp. His bold eyebrows and smooth face, so handsome. Amelia opened her mouth, wet her lips and prepared for a kiss. Her eyes begging and his grip tightening drew Amelia close. She liked the closeness and welcomed it by inching upward on her toes cautiously, to steal the idea of his impression close to her body. She pulled in heavily and began to pant softly. The sensation lingered and her body ached for his. Closer she pressed as her body became frantic. Amelia did everything she could to keep from reacting to her bodies' signals. Bob's eyes circled her face as if consulting every feature to memory.

"Frankly my dear, I don't give a damn,"

Bob said in a southern drawl.

Amelia blinked as if Bob had spoken another language. "What?"

"You know, Clark Gable, Vivien Leigh... Gone with the Wind, 1939." Bob said seriously.

His answered blurred Amelia's thoughts as Bob leaned over to kiss her. He coughed as if all the air had left his body. He released Amelia and backed away.

Leaning over, Bob tried to speak but his voice was hushed, little more than a dry, croaking whisper. "What cha' do that for?"

Amelia grabbed Bob by the collar and pulled him close to her face. His hands buried deep between his legs.

"Your ignorance is amazing." She said almost politely.

She tossed Bob across the room, deep into the pitch of shadows. She listened patiently for some of their collectibles to break his fall.

The room was once a mall of raw space. Now ancient avenues directed by large sculptures and breakfronts drifted towards the ceiling like seventh wonder gods. She looked at the clock. The witching hour was near.

An object, quick and soundless jetted by her. 'Maybe he had come back for me... Lucifer.'

The floor appeared to move beneath her feet, but the feeling suggested it came from above. Faint traces of casted shadows moved questionably along the walls. Amelia's imagination wasn't dulled by the idea that Satan had returned.

Her heart pounded heavily as she watched from the corner of her eye slight outlines shape a hidden dubious phantom. In other instances it would have been dismissed as sheer fantasy, something you thought you saw but didn't. Maybe even a mouse, creeping along the floor boards. 'Now that's sheer fantasy Amelia. Not logical at all. Collect your senses, it's him; Lucifer.' She thought.

Amelia dismissed the mouse; entirely. But it came back. First along the bottom of the wall and then her head. 'If this is a mouse, kill it... zap it. Do something, but whatever you do-do not show any signs of fear to him. He eats, drinks, and shits fear.' The thought made Amelia sick and she grimaced slightly holding her stomach. 'Tonight is his night; Satan. Sign the book.'

"No!" Amelia said defiantly. "I refuse."

"Give me another chance babe," Bob said. "or at least wait for me to ask."

Amelia spun around and saw Bob, floating ten-feet above the floor.

"You're floating." Amelia said surprised.

Bob smiled. "Isn't this great. I flew all the way here to surprise you, and to... to, uh...."

Amelia stepped into the light. The florescent, embedded in pebbled ovals overhead, seemed to be pushing in cycles, tearing through his flesh with pain and driving into his head. Bob's courage depleting, began to lose its highs as well as his altitude. He looked nervously around trying to appear in control but looking for words fitting her avid stare. 'Betty Davis eyes,' his thoughts urged him to put into a sentence. His feet touched the floor and his mind raced. The disk player clicked. He didn't realize how quiet the room was until the humming sounds of a turning wheel, the disk, spun to play another song. He imagined the laser seeking another tune to play at random and how Amelia's eyes would look once love had struck her again, here, in his arms. He was so close and like the stars that fell upon wishing eyes... 'Humprey Bogart and Lauren Becall.Katharine Hepburn and Spencer Tracy.'

"Fray Wray and King Kong." Bob said as if pushed; urged.

Amelia looked at him suspiciously. Bach's Sinfonia XI in G minor instrumental sonata form of classical music exploited his sound system. The clarity was stressed fully as the body of the pieces began to develop. The motivic material seemed to play through his body, moving him in some soul searching form. He threw out his hand that arched as if plagued with arthritis. Bob's face partially covered by his arm called to Amelia through scarlet eyes. Her body slacked then stiffened as suggested, and Bob, with a confident look, applied pressure.

Bob's voice was barely audible as he spoke. "Come to me... come to me Amelia."

She preceded closer, taking small gentle steps. Bob, almost losing composure, took in a deep breath and held it. The harmonic Sinfonia transformed contrapuntally through his body. Amelia stopped two feet in front of him. The translation in their eyes, near-perfect.

"Disrobe and bare to me the fruits of your loins." Bob suggested ambitiously.

He began to imagine her wearing a hosed-down ultra-sheer gown. Naked, but seeing nothing. She tugs at its sleeves over her hands, which stretches the neck and lets the straps of something black and lacy peep out.

"No way." Amelia said.

"Way Amelia, way!" Bob replied.

"Drop the Transylvanian accent," Amelia said evenly. "you're not Bela Lugosi and you're not from Romania. So why don't you just be yourself Robert."

Amelia turned laughing whole-heartedly.

"Take your clothes off." Bob said strongly.

Amelia turned on him again. An amused look on her face.

"Humph," Amelia said. "and what have you done for me lately?"

Bob took his cape off and threw it into the air. They watched as it floated to the floor squaring off into a make shift king size bed.

"I'm a right side man myself," Bob said. "but I'm flexible."

"What arrogance. Do most women fall for that line?" Amelia asked.

"Most." Bob replied.

He drew his sword. Amelia backed away sharply as if the double-edge crusader where a crucifix.

"I said take your clothes off." Bob said again.

"You do have nerve." Amelia scowled. "Is it your personality or your charm they surrender to?"

Amelia took another deep breath, her eyes never leaving the sword.

"Sixty-forty charm." Bob replied.

Amelia swallowed. "I think your charm is wearing as thin as your pompous one liner."

Bob realized that she was looking at the

sword and talking to him. Or maybe she was talking to the sword and waiting for it to answer her. Amelia was too stubborn to be afraid of anything and yet she appeared nervous, almost cynical. Bob waved it in front of his face and her eyes kept its pace. He stepped forward committing to an Olympic feint.

"En garde!" He yelled.

Amelia literally, to the word, jumped. Her back landing against a nineteenth century painting by Gauguin.

"Put that thing away." Amelia said nervously.

"Does it make you nervous Amelia?" Bob said enthusiastically. "Surrender or parish."

Amelia fell silent and Bob wondered if she thought he really meant it. He wanted to apologize and plead to her not to take his words out of context. But never was he in so much control.

Bob assumed a quarte parry position and sliced her gown from the neck, across her chest to her hip. Amelia saw the attack coming and closed her eyes. From his septime position he slashed across her waist then in an angle up over her left breast shearing the gowns shoulder then down to an overhead octave parry cutting through the center of her gown. The pieces fell to the floor like discarded ends of a seamstress.

Bach's Sinfonia began its last eight measures virtually duplicating the first eight as Amelia, maintaining a valid stand, opened her eyes. She was naked except for an entire sleeve to her shoulder and a loose piece of her silk gown covering her right breast. She wore a gold chain around her waist and a black silk fig leaf trimmed in gold cushioned between her thighs. Her legs were long and athletic with budding hips and a small waist. Bob raised the sword putting its razor edge against her inner leg. Amelia flinched. He gently ran the blade up her leg to her thigh giving her body the exact effect as if done with a razor blades edge. An ancient but currently used form of Japanese foreplay that intensifies hidden erogenous zones like the climax of a melody. She teetered pushing her head back against the painting. He pressed gently her secret part, giving warning of the silvers arrival. Bob's sense of touch was awakened by the swords advance, sending mental details to his mind, and it acknowledging Amelia's tenderness. He ran the point, making a grove in the silk, imitating the slit in her crouch barely touching the points of her desire, then pulling the blade away.

Amelia's eyes were closed, gathering the arousals of Bob's baitering and advancing them through imagination. Bob took the edge of the blade close to the tip and floated it over her exposed breast. Amelia turned her head away from the sword and the muscles in her jaws strained. Like silk, the blade touched her teat, going back and forth across it making Amelia's hands open then close tightly. Bob stepped back. He twirled the crusaders handle around his hand. It settled back into his palm and with one stroke cut the sleeve from the shoulder to the wrist. It too fell to the floor.

Amelia exhaled sending the shredded garment twirling like tornados in several directions. She looked at Bob, her eyes bright like a feline, trapped in a corner.

She pulled in an even breath. "Put that

damn thing away."

Beethoven's piano sonata in C sharp minor was the next selection. The timing was perfect. Bob lowered the sword to the side of his leg then let it drop to the floor. It fell slowly, striking the tarnished wood by the tip then falling gracefully with a hushed bobbling clink like a silver platter to thin carpet.

Amelia stepped hurriedly up to Bob and drew back a clinched fist. She looked at him with tight lips and drew her arm back further letting it go with blurring speed. Bob caught her attack by the wrist.

"A dear sweet woman," Bob said in a hushed voice. "who loves me and whom I love."

"What?" Amelia said in a quivering whisper.

Amelia's arm slacked and her hand opened. Bob kissed its palm.

"I love you Amelia." He said simply.

Amelia drooped as if to faint. Bob caught her, picked her up and carried her to the bed.

Ludwig Van Beethoven's Moonlight Sonata to his beloved countess continued as Bob laid Amelia down. He stretched her arms above her head and looked down at her tanned body. He held out his hand and pressed the palm. A razor sharp nail pushed through the tip of his index finger. Bob put it under the gold chain and with little effort set the silk leaf and gold free from her body. Bob knelt, lowering his face to her body, moved it over Amelia's chest and shoulder like a great grizzly before it dines. His breathe, inspiring against her essence, aroused Amelia's senses, making her body tingle.

Bob raised his hand in the air and the blades of every finger glistened in the lights. He clawed the veins of Amelia's wrist to forearm were injection and seduction begin. Amelia coughed gently, almost as if sobbing. Bob brought the razor shaped edges over her shoulder, across her chest and down to her stomach. He inhaled and exhaled close to her body, smelling her scent, faintly citrus. Bob parted her legs and looked up at Amelia.

"The blood is the life Amelia." Bob said softly. "But over and above all other cycles of life the true ethereal nexus of all things may only be sipped from the veins of another vampire."

He bowed between Amelia's legs and bit the inner right thigh.

"Ahhhh, la touche Bob." She managed to say pleasingly.

Her accent sprinkled over him like sugar over cafe au lait as the melody of the Saint Michaels' chime began. The grandfather clock bonged as the influence of gravity swung the pendulum freely like the striking of a sleeping heart.

Amelia's body changed forms from a hairy she-beast to an exotic ware-wolf. Her fangs grew as long as a saber-tooth tigers then retracting to the small bite of a night creature. Amelia's nails extended. She dug them deep into Bob's shoulders. He raised his head, blood dripped from his mouth like a wild animal. She looked down at Bob, her corneas burning like fire, exposed dilated pupils sparkling like a mirror reflecting the sun. Amelia pulled her nails from his shoulders and sunk the blades into her mouth. She lifted her hands, letting the blood drip into her mouth. Her tongue lashed out like a snake then circled around her nails and hands like a boa constrictor, growing in length and width. The clock struck its last romantic rhythm and her tongue withered back into her mouth. The nails were gone. The music stopped and the witching hour was upon them.

She gave Bob a sleepy smile. The morning after smile of satisfaction, peacefulness. The Scarlett O'Hara smile the morning after Rhett nailed her.

"Amelia, look." Bob lowered his head between her legs. "Hello, hello."

"What are you doing?" She asked as she pulled Bob's head up. "And why did you say that twice?"

"I didn't." Bob answered.

Bob was caught up in a hail of laughter and was unable to see the right cross coming. He flipped over several times hitting the wall with a heavy thud.

Bob looked over at Amelia. "You have no sense of humor."

"I'm laughing on the inside Bob." She smiled. "Well, gotta' fly."

Bob's eyes shot open. "Gotta' fly, GOTTA' FLY! What do you mean, gotta' fly? Where are you going?"

Amelia's feet dropped to the floor as she slid off the bed and walked towards a statue of Michelangelo's Dying slave.

Amelia turned on him. "I have no time to quarrel with you Bob." The evil in her eyes gave an impression of pure sass. "Trust me." She said definitely.

Bob picked himself up placed one hand on his back and popped it back into place. He walked over to his cape and thrashed it into the air. Bob fashioned the cape over his shoulders and clipped it closed around his neck. He ran to the stain glass windows throwing his body in front of the French pane as if blocking traffic. His head underneath the stained figure thought to be Muse Terpsichore.

"Over my dead body." He swore.

Amelia walked from the thrown shadow the stone statue gave, fully dressed. She strolled down the hall and opened the door. Bob ran after her. Amelia appeared again and went to the French windows. As she approached, they opened and she leaped out. Bob turned to intercept as the front door behind him slammed shut. He turned again and the windows locked with a click. Bob put his hands on his hips and stared at the stone slave. He scooped up his double edge crusader, twirled it around his hand and placed it into his open cape. Bob walked over to the French windows and opened them. He looked out into space sniffing at its ambiance.

Bob walked away from the open window, threw the cape around his body and it enveloped him. The cape opened, and again, Bob faced his fear. He ran towards the window and at its edge, dove out into the sprinkled darkness. He fell at an undetermined speed towards the ground. Bob tried to sweep upward from the dive by fanning open his cape but failed. He began to flutter like a broken winged pigeon and hit the ground expelling concrete and dirt into the air. Before the debris could settle, Bob jumped from the hole landing on his feet. He walked away from the scene as the bits and pieces of the street fell back around and inside the ditch.

Bob laughed comically, peering over his shoulder with a look as if cheating fate and fell into another hole made from a previous attempt at flight.

From the deep spoils of another Chicago pot hole, Bob swore again. "I hate it when that happens."

***

"You'll never believe what we've found Bridgette." Marcus said.

"You have the Com' Spock." The voice clicked.

"The satellite has picked up ectoplasmic readings. And it seems that this has happened several times today." Marcus said. "Why wasn't I told?"

"You said news worthy." The voice pitched. "Particle specks is not news worthy."

"Okay, okay." Marcus surrendered. "Let's start from go Bridgette. How were you able to get on line and decode a federal standard of encryption without the use of the computers?"

"This calls for the fifth amendment." The voice cracked.

"Bridgette." Marcus said annoyed.

The voice clicked twice before the words became recognizable. "Freedom of privacy act?"

"Be serious for once." Marcus said.

"If you insist." The voice answered back.

Marcus cleared his throat. "I insist."

"H..." The letter coughed from Bridgette's amplifier.

"H.... 'H' is nothing.   What's the 'H' for?" Marcus asked.

"It's good for a start." Bridgette said.

"A good start to what?" Marcus scratched his head. "As far as I know, 'H' does nothing."

The voice bleeped. "When it's followed by 'elp' it does."

"Elp!"   Marcus inhaled, and then exhaled. "You mean all you did was ask for help?"

The voice was plain excluding clicks, beeps or static. "Yes."

Marcus was stumped.   "From who Bridgette?"

The voice made an attempt at sighing. Thin track like arms rested on Bridgette's apparent hips. Bridgette had no mouth to speak of, but a grill type amplifier was placed just beneath a hole where the nose should have been.

"Basically," the voice sighed. "I needed a power boost so I plugged into the library and danced along the various megahertz spread spectrum that they're using to secure their radio chatter. Since I'm a mobile unit and your models are not, I've avoided an investigation by signaling help over cordless phones, cable systems, currently sophisticated black boxes, modems, and satellites. Basically everyone is getting the same information that you are without a direct connection to the source. Since the signal is digitized, making them unintelligible to humans, many people won't get it. And the ones that do probably won't understand it. And the last time I checked, I am neither human or anything close to it."

Marcus mulled this information over while facing the terminals that sat on a half circular table. He could look down at the key pad without moving his head. Marcus was locked into the one-piece shoulder mount and the slightest movement would pull anything broadcasting from a voyager launch to an episode of Archie and Edith Bunker.

Exact calculations had to be met. The wing-back, Bridgette, and the finest of technologies provided that. He was already at work bringing together the spirit world and the world of nature by way of scientific investigation. Marcus released the catch around his neck pushing the three-by six inch viewer towards the back of his head. The wing-back, now at a level of comfort, was aimed at the half circle of computer terminals.

Each phase of calculations was entered into separate pieces of hardware. And each calculation was measured numerous times per second until the outcome, approved by Marcus, was satisfactory; more than perfect.

"It's already plugged into the computer at Central which can pump out mind-boggling peek speeds of fifty-billion calculations per second." The voice signaled in digital and English. "That's hundreds of times faster than what you're perfecting. So why don't you link the two."

"Because users can access the electronic filing cabinet through Internet. If I do my calculations through STI, anyone can read my data-chats." Marcus replied without raising his head.

"But you're working on information that has already been accessed, processed, cleared and confirmed as accurate." The voice informed.

"I'm practicing on the new program I designed for the main frame computer." Marcus looked up. "And practice makes perfect."

He began to type again. This time with both hands.

Bridgette pulled the plug from the chromium skeleton that interlocked it with the library. Bridgette's ninety-eight pound frame, built as if thrown together from a child's box of assorted toys, lago blocks, train tracks and plastic odds and ends, rolled across the carpet silently on carbide balls.

"But all work and no play makes Jack a dull boy." The voice assured him.

"Bridgette," he said agitated. "I need to get this done."

"You promised to work on my neural network Marcus." The voice reminded him.

Marcus head jerked up. "This is important Bridgette."

Bridgette wheeled between him and the terminals. "You promised to work on my emotional option network.

"You're an AI." Marcus said. "You don't need emotions."

Bridgette turned as if to walk away. "Artificial intelligence systems attempt to replicate aspects of human intelligence. That term has fallen into disuse because early AI systems did not live up to their expectations."

"Who said that?" Marcus asked.

"You wrote it." The voice wheeled.

"But this is important Bridgette."

"Are you afraid of your emotions Marcus?" Clicked the voice.

"No."

The voice whirled and chimed. "Are you afraid to express your feelings?"

"Hell no!"

The voice held a touch of baritone. "Do I detect a note of hostility in your voice."

Marcus jumped up. The light weight shoulders mount taking him slightly forward.

"I am not hostile." He shouted, putting his hands, fist balled, on his hips.

"Remember Abby?" The voice asked rhetorically.

The room seemed to swell. Bright green cursor's blinked soundless, awaiting a command.

He unlocked the three-piece keyboard and placed it on the desk in front of the terminals. Marcus unfastened the shoulder mount and leaned it against the wing-back and sat down.

It had been years, and yes, Abby would get the attention that she'd deserve and Bridgette knew this.

He keyed in a command and sat back as the table rotated. A steady hum and a final click as a Macintosh terminal rested in front of him.

Marcus had been dreaming lately of Abby. She was dead now, found two blocks away; just dead. An autopsy showed two small wounds on the side of her neck and wrist and called it suicide. But he knew better.

In the years that came and went, he vowed to find this devil, this demon, and he did. Now with Bridgette's help he'd kill the beast that selfishly slaughtered his wife.

Through Bridgette he was to make a bridge between the scientific world and the occult.

He reached over and pulled the three-piece keyboard in front of him. Again, by the mere mention of her name, he went back. His eyes began to fill. Since her death, he dreamed of creating a video type photo album of Abby. But it just wouldn't do. With his Macintosh he created a three-dimensional virtually real replica of her. He labored secretly; meaning to surpass life's limits, and then came Bridgette.

Abby's mood swings and everything he knew, loved, and hated were stored on disks. But he wanted more. A fantasy better than VR. He built Bridgette and programmed

Bridgette to recall that name every time Bridgette thought he was neglecting his responsibility.

He placed his fingers on the home keys and looked up at Bridgette.

The eyes had to be dark enough to swallow an entire soul. The ears perfect shell sculptures. To create her, he thought to program unpredictability and enough mystery to scare him.

He started with hands, breast, nipples, bones, and muscles. This took five years.

To trap the evil that killed his Abby was a pain-taking program which took another eight. To trap him, he programmed one-thousand disks with an entire command of languages, psychologies, sociologies, histories, music; the works. Bridgette had to have quickness and be able to respond swiftly. Bridgette had to exceed his own wit or use it in a way to disarm a person. Be fearless, highly logical but a moral-a code, but not an opinionated one, and not one based on fear of an indirect effect. Bridgette's dialogue would mix formality and gutter language at the drop of a hat. He'd test it.

Marcus cleared his throat. "Bridgette, go fix me a cup of coffee."

"Who was your slave last week?" The voice cracked.

He was shocked and hid his amusement, but not surprised. Bridgette was programmed for that.

Bridgette had to love everything from Beethoven to rap. Her sexiness had to be so easy it hardly interested her. Her means of control would be the conscious effect of her body. That thought brought the Mac to life.

Marcus was astonished to find that his fingers took control while his mind wandered.

A two-dimensional view of how Abby would look on Bridgette came alive inside the Mac. He keyed in for perfection's as he was ready to start.

Her attitude had to be as perfect as her body. He didn't want to leave anything out. Bridgette would have to be the darling of frustration with a birth date. A mood plucked from the stars. He'd work on that later. A coded logic filter.

"Okay," Marcus said to himself, forgetting that Bridgette was still powered up.

"Feeling better big guy?" The voice asked clearly.

"Quite fine thank you."

"You know what I'd like for Christmas?"

The voice responded with a tone of unusual relaxation.

Marcus rounded his shoulders. "What would that be Bridgette?"

Marcus eyes, lost in the variations of his work, waited on a smart reply.

"Big breast and wide hips." The voice pitched.

The cursor rolled off the screen.

His face was wrinkled like balled paper. "Where do you come up with these things Bridgette?"

They replied in unison... "From the idiot box...."

Marcus hit the keystroke. Down the hall, the kitchen began to take on cross dimensions of a laboratory and Disney Land.

He thought of himself as Doctor

Frankenstein, but only for a brief moment. Piecing together body parts by means of graphic windows and a mouse. Bridgette's computer-aided-design had only been a list of digital codes. Speech, by the same means, a forged signature of a sound wave would now fool anyone.

The computer animation was ready. Marcus hit the keystroke playing it back into the computer's memory.

Bridgette's role model. Marcus thought about that one long and hard. His conclusion; she wouldn't have one.

Marcus brought up a list of Bridgette's programming: Neural Network stood out. To learn from past mistakes was a deep concern of Bridgette, but no longer his, as Marcus hit another keystroke making the report roll upwards on the terminal.

Headings appeared: Bioengineering, Robotics, and Bionics. His eyes rested on navigational system. He brought the program onto the screen by way of a keystroke. With another, unloaded it. There was just too much data to go over. The list continued: Weapons, he lifted his finger. Weapons, weapons, weapons. He had been working so hard he had almost forgotten about weapons and where to store them on Bridgette. He'd have to check that, and loaded the program.

"What will my brain look like?" The voice asked. "I can't imagine a chip big enough to store all the bytes of information you have on these disks."

"I'm not using silicon to make the chip." Marcus said, ignoring the blinking cursor. "I'm using Deoxyribo Nucleic Acid. That way they can duplicate themselves giving your neural net more brain power."

"We're talking major surgery here Sigman Freud." The voice churned. "I like the idea of you toying around with my body, I'm sure you've seen your share, but my mind. Did the cheese fall out of your sandwich or something? Hello, Earth to deep space."

"Don't worry." Marcus said, looking down into the terminal. A laser engineered arm stood out in red, green, and blue lights. "Hemoglobin is always in one or two states. It binds with oxygen and it doesn't bind with oxygen."

"Like an on and off switch."Churned the voice again.

"Exactly." Marcus replied looking up again.

"It sounds like a vacuum tube triode model SX70," The voice said. "the old brunt-out yes or no switches. Always overheating."

Marcus cleared his throat. "It's not like that at all Bridgette. Just calm down and let me finish. Actually, there's nothing wrong with what you have."

"If it isn't broke," the voice said smartly. "don't fix it."

The computers went down.

"Shit!" The word pressed through his teeth giving him a slight headache. "Bridgette, shut down everything I'm not using on this project. Reroute all power to the lab and this terminal."

"Yeah, yeah, yeah." The voice said smartly.

The Mac came to life again with the cursor blinking, awaiting another command. Marcus tapped the edge of the desk trying to recall where he left off. He raised both hands to his face and massaged roughly. He put both hands on the table, gripped its edge, and sighed.

Walking, as it were, Bridgette rolled on heavy-duty ball-bearing rollers. Besides the brain, being a natural pain to calculate, there has not been, to date, a two legged computer-controlled mechanical system to duplicate walking. The most stable walker devised was a six-legged system.

Upon studying Bridgette, he wondered how the servo-balancing weights throughout the frame would work. The weights would move throughout one-hundred different areas inside the framework giving Bridgette enough equilibrium to walk, run, jog, jump, and even stand on one foot without tumbling over. Still, it was an area of study. It would be years before Bridgette was to be let out into the real world. Just how Bridgette would react to that, he didn't know.

With a series of keystrokes, Marcus brought up Bridgette's programming list again.

The voice cranked itself up. "What will my skin feel like? Will it be smooth, supple and as soft as a baby's bottom?"

Marcus slammed a fist to the desk making the three-piece keying unit slid away from him. He twisted a palm into his forehead.

"Bridgette," Marcus said with a slight sigh. "you'll have flexible cells incorporated into tissue regenerated for burn patients."

"It sounds as if I'll be some sort of domestic all appliance type barefoot watch your mouth sunbathing house flunky." The voice clicked.

"Bridgette," Marcus looked up. "you'll

have nothing but the finest of everything. Trust me."

"I've heard that one before." Click.

"You haven't heard anything before. You haven't been anywhere." Marcus said.

"You'd be surprised." The voice replied.

"Look woman," Marcus said with a frown and a pointed finger.

The voice interrupted. "I'm not a woman, and I'm not a girl. Don't refer to me as a she, her or reasonable facsimile thereof. I have a name, and that name is Bridgette."

Marcus mouth hung open. His eyes blinked spasmodically then stuck; wide open. It was Abby.

"Will silicone breasts implants due," Marcus said. "size thirty-six?"

"Make them gel... size thirty-eight." The voice said evenly.

Marcus shook his head. A slight smile marked his lips as he sighed.

"Okay," Marcus said as he stood. "I think we're ready to begin."

With a keystroke, the lab, once a kitchen with mere convinces, doors opened. A condensed fog poured out as the sliding doors separated. It would be a seven hour operation in freezing cold temperatures. Marcus would have to observe through the observation windows as various sized medical robots and dozens of programmable universal manipulators assembled Bridgette.

"I think I'll wait until you're sure you're ready." The voice challenged.

"Bridgette," Marcus said in a tone that

meant, to them both, we're as ready as we'll ever be, and let's get on with this, continued. "just follow me."

Bridgette's make-shift legs lengthened to a full stand. Marcus walked towards the lab feeling that Bridgette was close behind.

The fog peeled around the edge of the doors, melting into the warm atmosphere of the living room.

Bridgette and Marcus stood inside the door looking into a page of a Hollywood science fiction movie.

There were rows of tubes running from bottle to bottle. An x-ray machine, monitoring system, six evaluation screens, life-support systems, a large black chair, and an electrocardiograph. From the corner of his eye he could almost see a glow across the face where the eyes will be. The range finder never left it.

"Okay," Marcus said. "hop on."

Bridgette looked at Marcus. "It's a bed."

"It's no ordinary bed." Marcus said.

Bridgette looked down at the bed then back at Marcus. "It's a Victorian bed."

"Yes it is." Marcus agreed. "I thought you'd be comfortable on this instead of a cold steel gurney."

"Take a look at me Marcus." The voice clicked. "A good look. Does it appear that I'm in need of comfort?"

"Just get in the bed Bridgette."

Bridgette rolled up to the bed and lifted the frame aboard.

"You're so forceful." The voice said inside the frame, and laid back. "I think I'm going to enjoy this." And Bridgette spread the frames legs open.

Marcus smiled, shook his head and walked away. The doors closed as he left.

PUMA arms reached across Bridgette as the fog began to build. With another keystroke, he had crossed a black hole with a machine.

5

Amelia watched Meribeth from deep inside the cemetery. It was ironically, across the street of the Sunshine Roller Rink where Meribeth stood in line for the Hollows Eve Ramble.

Amelia called out to her, and she,

Meribeth, knew of the calling as she heard it many times in her dreams and so strong the image of the intruder. It talked to her and took her to places where nightmares start, always asking the same question and giving out the same promises if she would sign the book.

Over the years due to her pact with the Devil, Amelia was forceful with others to do her bidding that is to sign the Devil's book. She mastered the art of manipulation promising them the same examples of money, silks, fine clothes, ease from labor and the chance to be rich and to live deliciously. But the best attack was to promote deep and uncompromising envy. Closely associated with anger, the two motives formed a kind of tandem-malice and envy. In part, a woman was so angry because she was so envious she was therefore easily persuaded to covenanting the possessions and advantages of others. Woman were needy, and greedy, and forever determined to get what they wanted. If they didn't get what they wanted they wouldn't hesitate to resort to stronger means; witchcraft.

Amelia took the steps further. As affliction was a direct manifestation of her power and not Satan's, she maintained and controlled others who in fact brought heads of office to their knees as they were weak for the flesh of those women possessed. Presidents in scandal, priest, influential members of congress and kings of nations. Even in the beginning of Popes I through VII Amelia dealt out the most powerful of women flesh peddlers into gaining over men to admitting their own temptations, bringing them further into Satan's welcome.

Battles, wars, enmity, blood-shed, slaughter and the destruction of mankind was supported by her, in quest of a hand of some maiden or damsel in the form of distress fabricated by Amelia and the sinful, unruly passions her insignificant lot possessed.

At times, the Devil-like passions that enhanced the letting in of Satan and his temptations seemed all too easy. She felt he knew and let her run her course endangering others to the horrid sin of covenanting with him.

Each Sabbath, Amelia would collect heavily the souls so due. She had one last sacrifice to collect and soon she comes. A virgin for the Druids All Hollows-Eve festival.

As an intruder, Amelia embraced a very large theme. It was as if Amelia and her victim were battling back and forth across a vital territory with boundaries assuming the greatest possible significance. On this level Meribeth labored strenuously to keep Amelia at a distance, while she, for her part, was forever thrusting in. Counter-magical strategies designed to establish clear and impermeable boundaries where Meribeth would place odd artifacts near her threshold to keep Amelia away. Such things as bay leaves or horseshoes. At this level of fantasy, the same theme was powerfully evident and countered.

Time and time again Amelia attacked Meribeth at home and in bed, coming through the window or in at the keyhole.

There was no way to prevent Amelia from gaining whatever access she desired. Soon there was no part of Meribeth that was beyond reach. Her private conversations as well as her thoughts were known to Amelia.

Also embarrassing events in the past and important prospects of the future. The most dramatic forms of reach by Amelia of victimization was outright possession of Meribeth's wants, needs and desires; her dreams. Amelia dictated the details of Meribeth's behavior. Without word, Amelia attacked.

As Meribeth slept, in a distraught state of Amelia's haunting's, Amelia entered her dreams.

Meribeth was there, in a spotlight in her mind. She could feel and hear footsteps approaching.

Her body and vision trembling with each echoing step. Amelia appeared, wearing a black one piece sweat suit that looked as if it were painted on.

"Got a cigarette?" Meribeth asked looking nervously around.

Amelia only stared. Meribeth coughed then gagged. A cigarette was pushed from her mouth. She fumbled it suspiciously between two fingers while the tip of the cigarette sat uncomfortable between her lips.

Meribeth swallowed. "Got a match?"

A stiff brow raised above Amelia's right eye. A complete double of Meribeth'sself appeared next to her.

"I meant a light..." Meribeth choked down a dry swallow. "for the cigarette."

Amelia snapped her fingers. The body

double ignited by the feet raising to consume her body. She stood quietly as the flames singed the body-double's face and touched her hair. Meribeth leaned over and lit the cigarette. The fire went out and the charred carcass fell to its side crumbling to ash.

Meribeth began to tap her left foot. She took a deep pull from the cigarette and exhaled in Amelia's direction.

Feeling relaxed, and a bit settled, "Got an ashtray?" Meribeth asked.

"You're standing in it." Amelia replied. "Will you be needing anything else? Panties, bras, a box of extra strength tampons for those sizeable wounds?"

"What sizeable wounds?" Meribeth swallowed.

Amelia spat on her. Three inch leaches

appeared where the spittle rested sucking and burrowing into her skin.

"SHIT!" Meribeth screamed.

Meribeth patted herself pulling a leach from her skull.

"You bitch." Meribeth shook what was left of the leaches from her face. "I'm tired of your stupid fucking games. Why don't you just leave me alone?"

And she flicked the butt of the cigarette into Amelia's face. It spun through the air, slowly. Its glowing end hit then soaked into Amelia's cheek. The left eyebrow rose, equaling the right.

"You..." Amelia chastised. "you with your proms, girl scout badges, dates. I've little value, nothing of worth to call my own. So I'll take this difference from you, and take it with me. Like so many immoral women whose thoughts, hidden from rational thinking on the dark side of the mind-sup with the living. Now it's time to dance with the dead."

"What do you want from me?" Meribeth asked.

"Sign the book Meribeth," Amelia screamed sadistically. "and carry out your viciousness towards those who are apt to harm you. You are a perfect instrument for Satan."

Meribeth managed a dry swallow. "Is my life in your hands or his?"

Amelia stepped closer.

"Give your blood to him and your answers and wishes will be fulfilled. Be ready to die, and to die you must be reborn. Sign the book and this be all the magic." Amelia promised.

"Who are you?" Meribeth asked.

"I'm your audience. The object of your strength. Take this symbol of your destructive impulses."

Amelia offered her an empty hand. But in Meribeth was a bill-hook.

"Murder your parents..." Amelia suggested.

Meribeth's body stiffened.

"your neighbors..." Amelia's eyebrows pierced to a frozen frown.

Meribeth held the hook in her hands surveying the polished iron counting obvious reasons to argue Amelia's devious approach.

"Or how about those young boy's..." Amelia looked for a response. "yes, throw them into the fire. Serve him faithfully and he will not refuse you."

"You want to kill me too?" Meribeth said

that deep groveling entanglement of pebbles and fermented juices in her voice, straining up an octave.

Amelia stepped closer. The sounds of her persuasion bouncing off the soft walls of Meribeth's mind.Her sleeping form resting.Her eyes moving rapidly about in a dream.

Amelia pushed further. Her voice soothing and comforting as she sympathetically stroked Meribeth's hair.

"Agree to a contract of your own choosing." Amelia suggested.

Amelia raised a pawl from her side. There was a chain through the center and five holes around that which her fingers sat comfortably. She grabbed Meribeth's hand exposing her wrist. The notches of the device were razor sharp as she lowered it to Meribeth's arm.

The clash of the bill-hook intercepted the razor edges of the pawl.

"Screw you!" Meribeth spat.

Amelia smiled. "You are weak towards him. Satan. You're courage deceives you. Your patience misleading you. You are displeased, more malicious and so more apt to revenge. Covenant with him now..."

Amelia raised the glistening edges of the pawl high in the air.

"SIGN THE BOOK." Amelia shouted.

The bill-hook was sunk deep into Amelia's chest. She stumbled backwards as the blood rushed over her body. Amelia touched the hook and looked up at Meribeth, the pawl raised high above her head. She pulled the pawl back and threw it at Meribeth. It spun in the air causing sparks like a dangling muffler from a speeding car. It sliced through Meribeth's shoulder. Amelia pulled at the chain causing it to spin back to her like a boomerang aimed at Meribeth's neck. She ducked under it. The links receding into Amelia's sleeve. She caught the pawl by its edges and lowered her hand to her side. A continuing flow of linking metal fell to the soft pulp of a floor from her sleeve.

A whispering shot, a sound so hushed like a bullet from a silencer sped just as swiftly cutting the links close to Amelia's fingers. Amelia studied each finger carefully and without looking up saw Meribeth holding a horseshoe in her hand. Another horseshoe magically appeared as Meribeth, amused in sleep, wasted no time sending the sharpened projectile in Amelia's direction. The first embedded itself in Amelia's skull. The next into her left breast. Dozens were thrown sending Amelia retreating into the dark.

She had won. The nightmares were over. Meribeth wondered how she could leave. She contemplated the situation and smiled reassuringly. 'All I have to do is wake up.' She thought.

She heard the scrapping sounds of metal against metal. In the distance she could see the fiery sparks of the pawl and the chain. She turned and ran. The act appeared to be to no avail as she knew there was no where to go.

Meribeth faced the conspiracy with what little courage she had left. The flaming disc was closer than she thought, and not aimed at her. It hit the soft walls cutting at its pulpy tissue. Meribeth fell to her knees clutching her head in pain. As her sleeping self, the throbbing was agonizing. She clawed at her face and into her eyes trying to get in to stop the sharp stabs of an over-powering migraine. She forced a scream and sat up. Her night gown, sheets and pillow soaked in sweat. She was hyperventilating and put a hand to her chest.

"It's over, it's over now. No more." Meribeth chanted.

She looked around her room. It was fashioned in pink and lace with dolls and stuffed animals thrown about in a orderly clutter. Her friends, the silent companions of her youth. Her desk, window-sill and floor were covered with them. They frightened her. She was tempted to throw them out into the yard.

Her attention shot to the door, then the clasp locking the window. She gasped again but this time in relief to see it securely locked. She grabbed a pink elephant and pulled it close to her. A final look around her room made her feel at peace. Her eyes settled on a family picture. She'd dream about that now and fell back into the awaiting comfort of her pillow. Moments later she was asleep.

Her eyes shot open. She could hear the distinctive sounds of someone walking or the heavy pounding on a wall. But she was awake. The fear of another confrontation was weak... void. But premature as the ceiling opened. Amelia fell on Meribeth's chest. The horseshoes pinned in her body and face like an awkward chitin.

"I will make you afraid before I am done with you." Amelia denounced tactfully.

Amelia raised the pawl and aimed for Meribeth's throat. Meribeth threw herself from the bed. Stumbling blind for an exit, she ran down the steps across the spacious living room and opened the front door. She stood in the lemon light of the open door. Her breathing cut through all other nocturnal sounds. The shrill of the cicadas drowned out evidence of a beating heart. In her haste she realized that she was without a coat. She made an attempt to enter the house. Foot prints pressed deep into the carpet as if someone were creeping up on her walked cautiously down the steps. She backed into the doors frame, turned and jolted down the long flight of flag-stone steps realizing the dream was just too strong.

She wandered for hours until she found herself in a field. The crushing of dried leaves edged her to take refuge in a nearby shack. A dark lone figure moved amongst the tall dry weeds. It entered the shack closing and latching the door behind it.

"I know you're in here." A cool eerie voice

said.

She hid behind the left tire of a late model tractor. It was machine green but in the stale light everything was marveled in gray. Meribeth closed her eyes and pictured herself there, inside her mind.

It was the same as she remembered: cold, poorly lit with savage rips and tears in what appeared to be the brains tissues. Her head began to churn, instant stabbing to her temples. She didn't know what to call her. She just called out. The agony intensified with each cry. It was no use. She wasn't asleep but turned to walk away. Meribeth tilted forward as if pushed.

"You frightened me. I uh... agree to a contract." Meribeth said.

The horseshoes and bill-hook caved into Amelia's body leaving large gaping wounds.

"A contract between two friends huh." She continued.

Amelia's wounds disappeared as she folded her arms.

"Okay... you give me five years and I'll serve you... uh, I mean him," Meribeth waved her hand. "who ever. And make me a witch and all that other stuff and I'll sign your stupid book. Okay, is that a deal or what?"

Meribeth held her hand out. Amelia turned and walked away.

"There you are bitch. Mumbling in the dark like an old woman." The voice said.

Meribeth's eyes sprang open. The dark figure grabbed her by the shoulders and slung her into a mound of dried straw. The screams were muffled; imaginative, as if she were being choked.

A shadow emerged from the badly weathered shack completely naked. It stepped into the rays of the moonlight. Blood dripped from its mouth as it raised both arms to the sky as if it had just awakened holding something small and foreign.

"I did it. I nailed her and it was good." He said.

A lamb walked from behind the shadow. The shadow resembling a male figure flinched slightly as the wool brushed against his leg. The lamb looked both ways nervously wobbling on thin legs as if shot. A chorus of laughter from the tall thin blades of grass and weeds startled the timid sheep. It jumped, then darted like a wild bucking horse before it ran off behind the shack and into a clearer part of the field.

The stranger examined his self and the

contents in his grasp. Blood soaked his thighs and genitals. Balls of gray wool filled his palm as he opened his hand.

"I had her... I had the whore right here. In the barn. She's in here. I know it." He said firmly.

He stepped inside to what was now brightly lit by kerosene lanterns. There was nothing and no one there. No need to search or look around. She got her wish.

But she, Meribeth, wanted other things such as success at skating, popularity and control over men. She was granted these meager wishes for her virginity and to do Amelia's bidding, sign the book.

Amelia was to collect as Meribeth was now twenty-one and her five year reign was to this night at end.

Amelia silently called out to her again from deep inside the cemetery. Meribeth stepped from the slow moving line in front of the roller skating rink and into the spotlight of a street lamp. Amelia increased her telepathy, commanding Meribeth to drop her bag. She wore a bright orange sweater two sizes too big which drowned her hands and body to her knees. Her black hair flowed over her shoulders with strands falling over her eyes.

She walked out into traffic. Cars and trucks avoided a collision with inch-clearing accuracy and tire-squealing aplomb around her. The people along the wall watched in awe but casually understood it as another means of childish attention. 'It's only Meribeth,' her popularity increasingly dull now by her many strange attempts to reach it.

Meribeth reached the other side and stood in

front of the cemetery gates waiting for them to open. Amelia pressed her thoughts further and Meribeth walked through them. The bars pushed her back as her body melted around the rusted poles then joined together on the other side.

Four young boys hidden in the gold of maples, the crimson of oak and sumac watched the rusted poles split Meribeth's body in several slices. A hallucination that should have sent them to secrecy.

The haze of the rich colors of autumn, the neon lights, black and green crepe-paper were a perfect explanation of distorted reality.

John, the oldest of the group was eager at playing a last minute game. The others were convinced that it wasn't the time or place because of what they thought they saw but quietly kept it to themselves.

"This is our chance to get that stuck up bitch Meribeth." John said.

John shot the challenge at the wide eyed bunch. They were crotched until he stood over them, making his challenge more intimidating. He was slender from the waist down with broad shoulders, fair skin and sandy-brown hair. His eyes reflected strength and shyness. A perfect characteristic for someone of twenty. But the half smile, half sneer was all that really was needed to spark the others interest. All except Jason who needed more encouraging.

"I think we should just go to the grocery store like we planned and punch holes in the milk cartons." Jason said unsure of himself.

Jason was the youngest, but not too young. He was seventeen and a half he would always say adding the extra six months as if it gave him an excuse or right to drink and stay out late with the other three. He could never hold his liquor, and when they weren't looking, dumped it.

Bobby and Phil stood up next to John, making him appear even taller; majestic.

"Screw that sissy crap," John spat. "either you can come with us or sit your sorry ass here."

Bobby, Phil and John laughed as special emphasis on the word 'come,' was now immortalized. A statement they'd childishly treasure.

They turned running for the gate. The dried leaves becoming crushed reminiscences of a season gone by echoed beneath their feet like the whisper of children. Jason hesitated. He pushed the sparse limbs of a bush aside to watch.

Meribeth's body joined together on the other side bringing her out of her trance. Jason felt that it wasn't the streamers or lights but Meribeth who was playing tricks again. John just couldn't get enough. It would have been rape then and the humiliation came when a farmer's sheep leaped from the shed. The screams were unreal and John, after weeks of ridicule confessed that it was the lamb who screamed and not Meribeth. He vowed to teach her a lesson and forced Bobby, Phil, and himself to help. Although John made it appear as if they wouldn't have it any other way, Jason agreed only to act if and when Meribeth needed his help but was still too afraid of John. As they approached Meribeth he somehow feared for them. A deep fear for their lives.

Meribeth." John yelled.

She turned around but Amelia intercepted her thoughts and words.

"You want to finish that game?" John asked.

"What game is that John? Would it be by chance that you're searching to find your roots in the animal world? There are no sheep here, try again." Meribeth said calmly.

Phil and Bobby howled with laughter. John threw his hands to his side like a gun-slinger and the laughter stopped. John grit his teeth until his jaws ached. She was taunting him again. Making a fool of him. It was a joke that followed him through school that he swore would end.

"Real funny Beth. What you say me and my two friends..." At that point Jason came running up behind them. "Make that three friends," John continued. "Screw you until you scream."

"And what do I get?" Meribeth questioned.

It was a response not likely given and John rounded his mouth and eyes as if it were his last chance at a ten-thousand dollar prize.

Amelia could not ward them off with the idle thoughts of Meribeth. She invited them in.

"If you can catch me then I'm yours for the night." Meribeth teased.

Meribeth plucked the cold iron of the bars. She ran her hand back and forth across them. The sound was that of a train moving on tracks. They were hypnotized by her movement. The bars began to glow an emerald green. In their fascination, her fingers against the wrought iron fence became a dead quiet as if the train had come, gone and now passed on into silent darkness. They failed to notice Meribeth walking away. With her back turned to them she spoke in a sweet and luring tone.

"Coming?"

Meribeth was thirty feet into the cemetery. The area was a plot of extensive acreage. A few wild spruce, red wood and oak positioned off by hundreds of marble stones. Light raindrops began to fall tapping the dried leaves as if someone were balling up paper.

They stared at Meribeth's back through the glowing green bars, unsure and definitely scared. They looked over at John only to see what appeared to be sweat beading the top of his forehead and etching down the side of his face. Meribeth turned on them. Amelia selfishly inpatient.

"Or are you scared?" She challenged.

John's cheeks stiffened and he stepped through the gates. A fog had all but consumed her but he could see her silhouette.

Amelia applied pressure and Meribeth responded. She walked deeper inside the cemetery with John searching frantically behind her. He called out from his dark corner to Phil who jumped through the bars. Bobby was next, pulling himself in and out marveling at the emptiness of the gates center trying to put to memory the strange ringing sounds made as his body passed through the middle. Phil pulled him through and they headed off in separate directions.

Jason stepped back shaking his head from side to side as the invitation to him, unnatural. Was he the only one who had sense to realize that you just can't walk through iron bars. But they did.   And if he didn't, the world, according to John, would be written on the sides of buildings, sidewalks and maybe even his mothers garage labeling him a sissy; nerd.

He walked up to the bars; his hand trembled as it passed through. His mouth was dry as he swallowed. The cold wet rain was soothing in sound as it vastly began to powder his face. He stepped through but it was too late. The iron had formed to solid trapping his body in pain gripping confusion. A single bar stuck through the nape of his neck piercing his lungs and out through his back-side freezing him in a statue like pose. His left hand was wrapped around the cold sting of the gate. He could feel the chill of the iron leave the bar and into his palm. The thought of telling them to wait for him stuck in the center of his chest. He was aware of each breath. Inhale. Exhale. He wondered how many breaths he had left.

Phil's view was like looking through a cars tinted window from the outside. He spit the distance of four yards onto a tombstone. He took much pride in coughing up a degree of mucous and placing it where his eyes were leveled. The spittle hung loose over large RIP initials. He stopped and brushed it off with the bottom of his shoe. The top part of the stone read: Good husband and provider.

Phil was the arrogant type. All he needed was a push in the wrong direction. He looked not wider than he was long, like a basketball player wearing an army crew-cut and plain brown eyes. He giggled and laughed at everything. Even the suffering of strangers and the agony of friends. But alone a different Philip Houston would escape the strains of peer pressure. The pressure he felt when he'd hear a knock at the door or a tap on his basement window where he slept. To him John was his nemesis as well as his hero. Sometimes he'd push just enough, and sometimes Phil just wanted to be left alone.

He unzipped his pants and urinated on the stone slab. It appeared stained then dried with each slight turn of his hips.

Meribeth had come up on Amelia passing her and saying nothing. Amelia was in route to meet with her friends almost failing to realize the differences. It was a brief change of thought as each of them with the dramatics of a time piece turned and met each other.

Meribeth's eyes were egg-shell white as Amelia gripped her face with a strict hand. Smoke emerged from somewhere deep inside Meribeth, covering Amelia's hand like a dense salve. Amelia's eyes, a murky black with glowing otter rims like an eclipse showed a legitimate breach of morals, a disruption of her soul.

She pulled Meribeth closer, gripping her powdery white face with such pressure that she responded wildly flinging her arms and clutching at Amelia's wrist as if the pain had warded off the effects of Amelia's spell. Amelia pushed her off her feet. Her back hitting the cold earth with a heavy thud.

Amelia assumed the likeness with her malignant touch soaking the features that confined Meribeth to a gentle attraction... now lethal.

She walked up behind Phil startling him. He turned on Meribeth. The last pressurize strains of relief soaked her patent leather wedge shoes. He giggled, and then laughed shaking his loose member as he teetered. No sooner did the last few drops hit the packed soil beside her feet that Phil was heaved high into the air. He hit his head on the ground. A flash spun around inside his head like explosions from fire-works. He imagined how it felt to be too close to a fire-cracker.

"You found me now do me." A voice high above him said.

Phil's eyes adjusted to the concussion. Meribeth stood over him.

"I'm all yours girlie." He chuckled.

She easily squatted over him, running her hands from his crouch to his stomach as he watched. She laid her hands on his shoulders pressing her body between his legs. He pulled in a deep breath closing his eyes. He could smell her breath and the heat of it coming closer to his mouth. She kissed him. Her tongue engaging in artful twist and turns with his. Phil's mouth began to fill up with the hot soothing passions of her excited glands. Saliva dripped from the corners of his mouth. The weight on his chest; enormous. He forced his head back turning it to get a better look. The white mucous from her mouth began to foam and pour from her mouth in waves. Phil tried pushing her off him but it was no use as each shove and every word forced him deeper inside the dirt. It spilled from the openings in her nose, ears, and the corners of her eyes. Warm spittle washed over him closing off air passages until he drowned in it.

A svelte Meribeth walked through the cemetery donning only her sweater. Her bare feet across the lawn had a certain magical connection with the earth. To Bobby she appeared to be moving in jerking motions as if he closed his eyes too long, she'd appear in another place, still coming towards him.

He sat nursing a can of beer feeling the contents of the can bubble inside him. 'It's a man's thing' they'd say as they would each try to outdo one another's sonic gurgle from somewhere deep inside their lungs.

Bobby looked like a carnivore and a drinking man by the size and shape of his stomach. With his face turned away and looking at the side of his frame, one would suggest two weeks to a month due. He had a severe girth appearing to have lived as well as a man of fifty but too attenuated for his own good. A gaseous outburst was forming just as Meribeth reached for his shoulders.

"Ready?" Meribeth asked soothingly.

Bobby belched in her face. Meribeth stepped back raising the soppy sweater exposing pink nipples and trimmed pubic hairs. The beer can fell to the ground. He belched again.

"Damn right!" He said.

He grabbed both breasts with his hands squeezing their firmness. Meribeth lowered her sweater over his head and pulled it down over his body. It was warm inside the cotton fabric and her skin moist as if dried from a shower. He was being pulled closer as the sweater around him tightened. He kissed her softly, smelling the warmth of her body. His breathing became flashes of short gasps as the distance between them closed. He became frantic with the idea of wanting to be inside her as his hands fumbled in darkness causing a lustful friction. Bobby reached between her legs. The warmth there was desirable as two fingers rubbed then pierced the moist area. He dug three fingers in splitting her to what should have been to her stomach. The sweater tightened making it almost impossible to move freely. His imagination began to get the better of him, but the reality of his passion demanded relief. Bobby unfastened his pants and reached around her sealing the distance. He grabbed her rear squeezing the flesh in both hands thinking that they were too soft for a woman with such shapely breast. He pulled her closer to him pushing deep with each pelvis thrust until his hardness was in his hands. She was gone leaving a residue over his body. The sweater continued to hold him, consume him, making the air clammy and earthy. A recognizable stench filled his nostrils. He managed to put a hand to his nose creating a pungent order. He gaged then coughed. The sweater tightened for the last time as his body began to fold. Something or someone pushed him downward. He spoke aloud. A sound that he should have heard but didn't. There was no sound-only silence.

His feet felt as if they were dangling from a high position. His face and lungs began to burn just as he was pushed again. Only half a second passed as his body hit a pool of water. The clear air and cool water was an instant relief but the stench remained. He was going down for the third time reaching for the light above him. A log brushed by him and he grabbed for it with one hand then both. He wrapped his arm around the cut timber shaking the water from his eyes. The light above him blinking like a florescent light bulb about to go out. His eyes batted frantically as he wiped the water from his face hoping it would clear his mind as well.

The night had been a complete blur of mishaps and unanswered incidents. He shook his head pressing a palm to his eyes. Bobby was sure the beer was playing tricks on his mind. Looking up into the blinking light he swore he saw a man's privates. The light became a piercing laser, then a flooding white. He heard words which echoed all around him. All he could see was white. And all he smelled was a familiar waste.

The words became clear. A sound he recognized that was etched in his mind forever. It was, to him, impossible. His father was dead, but he heard his loud audible voice. He looked up again. His father's weather beaten face looked down at him, as large as a bill-board along the road of a highway.

"You're a piece of shit," the voice said. "and that's all you'll ever be."

Bobby gripped the log so hard it split in two. He went under for the last time as the lid to his watery tomb fell shut. The chime of the pulled handle and the whirling mechanics of the basin pounding in his ear as he was pulled into the drain.

John heard the screams followed by laughter. In the wide open space of the cemetery it was hard to tell just where it came from and who was doing what.

He was the kind of person when asked to taste spaghetti sauce claimed he didn't like tomatoes. But every Friday night would hoard an entire pizza to himself making him either cleaver at concealing from others what he really liked or just plain ignorant.

A hand reached around John grabbing his privates with a gentle touch. He jumped slightly then moved curiously against the firm caresses.

"This cock big enough for you Beth?" John asked.

"If it were any bigger I'd be renting you out stud." She replied.

She turned John around. His eyes trying to read her thoughts. She placed an open palm over his crotch rubbing its length.

John's body stiffened. "Is it hard enough for you?"

"Hard enough to drive a rail-road spike through a two-by-four." Meribeth said.

She squeezed it. The pressure pleasurable at first then painful. He wrapped both hands around her waist gritting at the teeth. Her expression never changed as the sound of crushed gristle pushed out at his ears. John fell to his Knees. His eyes pressed together causing a severe headache. He looked down between his legs. His hands creating more pain it seemed then the actual cause, which to him was unreal. But the dark fluid over his knuckles proved an act had been executed. The misery to look up into Meribeth's eyes was nothing compared to the pain felt in his bowels as the stained flesh held in her hands was shoved into his mouth. He fell backwards; full of himself.

A natural blush washed over her face. "Smoke if you have them."

Meribeth looked over her shoulder and realizing where she was couldn't believe how it was possible and why.

Amelia commanded her again, and again Meribeth responded. She walked up to Amelia and looked into her eyes. They were that of a cat in the dark and Amelia brushed the hair from over her eyes demanding better control.

Her blush features and brown eyes were unwavering and again Meribeth asked. "Is my life in your hands?"

Without words, Amelia circled Meribeth's face with a finger and waved her eyes closed.

Amelia was too powerful and could feel a surge dominating each thought stricken spell cast.

A hand-sized golden orb spinner rested on Amelia's shoulders. The spider sealed the last silk thread to her gown that made it stronger than steal, more elastic than nylon and tougher than a bullet proof vest. She needed all the energy possible and the spiders silk was a rare absorber. Harvesting and controlling them took the basic knowledge of magic which she possessed.

The spider crawled over her body examining her and tightening each thread.

From her sleeve she pulled out a chain with

the Ankh symbol of reincarnation and placed it around Meribeth's neck. Amelia whispered to Meribeth.

"With this is to worship RA, the God of Egypt, Lucifer. In order to worship him," She continued. "in his rites, you will give up your virginity and practice orgy's."

Meribeth opened her eyes. The pupils gone as if erased. Amelia handed her a shovel. "Dig!"

And without question, Meribeth began digging. Amelia again pulled, from her sleeve, a compact. She opened it and in seeing her reflection, smiled. The compliment was premature as Amelia's features began to wrinkle. The black lip stick on her lips began to peel as her lips dried. She touched her cheek and her hand was without flesh as she stared consciously into a nightmare. A finger broke, dangled, then fell off. Amelia looked back into the mirror and her face began to drip like melting plastic. Her eyes sunk deeper and deeper into their sockets until she was blind. She pulled in a deep breath as if to release a scream but couldn't. It was stuck there and swelled. At this point she thought she would explode... and she did. The thought and her actual blindness served as some type of warning as Amelia opened her eyes and senses to the sounds of metal against wood. She looked directly into the mirror and the look of one-thousand years loomed back. Amelia slammed the compact shut and without moving her head looked around.

Meribeth kept digging, scrapping the wooden coffin with the shovels point, slinging it over her shoulder as if she were still pulling up dirt.

Meribeth stopped, but not by her power, and climbed out of the ditch. Amelia, sensing nothing, climbed in. She looked the length of the casket and assuming the area of her desires dove a stiff hand through the wood and pulled out the occupants head. Amelia held it up to the sky as if it were an offering then brought it down to her face. It was a freshly decaying skull of a man, grey, moist and reeking resins left behind by lack of atmosphere. Its skin hung loose over Amelia's fingers as she began to gnaw off bits of the dead man's face.

Meribeth stood at attention, unmoved by the sight. She still held the shovel customary to the formal line of the military. Her eyes, ghost white.

Amelia ate her fill and raised the skull to the sky again, then dropped it back through the hole of the coffin. She climbed out of the hole and stood in front of Meribeth. Her eyes closed, Amelia backed away. Meribeth fell to her knees, her head shaking out of a daze. She looked at Amelia then down inside the ditch. A question marked Meribeth's face in the shape of a frown as she looked up towards Amelia. A hand, long and bony reached from the grave and pulled Meribeth in.

Amelia, satisfied, folded her arms. She watched the cars pass outside the gates under the large sign that read: ALL HOLLOWS-EVE RAMBLE.

A funnel formed in the clouds above Amelia. Dirt was tossed into the air spinning like ashes swirled in the dregs of coffee.

The sky cracked creating miles of endless blue streaks. The air was rich with the freshness of a warm October. Almost too warm but attractive enough to be called an Indian summer.

Amelia smoothed back a wayward wisp of

daring brunette hair feeling the spray of an upcoming shower. The hint of a smile at the corner of her now blue-green eyes weakened as a sharp cramp arose in her stomach. She doubled over leaning helplessly against a tree. A bolt of lightning fell like a two-ton weight near her shattering a headstone in numerous chalky pieces. Savoring nature as it were, Amelia pulled in a full even breath straightening from the inhalation of a moist atmosphere.

A darting ray of light slow enough because of the distance came powering down towards Amelia. The anesthetized blow from the clouds hurled her into a subtly camouflage of brush. The gown soaked all its power as she stretched crucified amidst the twisted branches.

From the corner of her eye she mistakenly

saw a figure standing on top of the south wall of the cemetery. It was quite dark at that distance and could naturally be the top of a statue, a monument over a grave. But to her thoughts she could not be sure if it was always there. She watched the shadow as she again, perceived him to be here... but who?

The gnawing of a dead man's flesh was a tradition used in order to take flight. She walked on the nightmares and fears of those so easily persuaded to covenant with Satan; to sign the book. Her efforts this night was to join her clan to celebrate the most festive of Sabbaths.

She passed through the visible, to some,

half of the great circle that passes through the zenith and the celestial poles. The familiar subdivision of the day into twenty-four hours, the hour into sixty-minutes, and the minute into sixty-seconds is of ancient origins to which the time bearers, Satan's demons, had much control of until AD 1600. Amelia used a much simpler means. She just changed the hands of the grandfather clock to Greenwich time making the timing of the witching hour simpler to her and confusing Bob completely.

Greenwich Time defined by scientific began at midnight rather than noon. Universal time, the principal scale and effects, leap years, and seconds all were too confusing to control and understand as it were. His, Satan's, majority was educated directly on magic and destruction.

The synodic month, the interval from new

moon to new moon was Satan's happiest. And tonight, ALL HOLLOWS-EVE, the moon was raised high. His holiest of Sabbaths and the returning of his soul to Earth in flesh was to be celebrated this day and all not present would bare his wrath.

The 29.531 days it takes for each new moon to new moon, took one-thousand years to reach this solar day. The festival would last forever and a day as he would celebrate by persuading men and women to throw their children into the fire bringing about their eventual destruction.

The significant rising and setting of the sun and moon reinforced the popular belief of the sky worshipers of the temple of Stonehenge. Amelia's destination was Salisbury Plains. The relic of prehistoric Britain; Stonehenge.

***

Bob walked back into his apartment and slammed the door. He sneered at the 3rd century five-foot marble statue of Venus De Medici and kicked it as he passed.

The 5th century bronze warrior, the nine foot marble workings of Michelangelo Buonarroti's the Awakening Slave, the song (sung) dynasty's 12th century wood covered seated Guan Yin and the over life-sized marble pieces of the Three Goddesses, all headless, were lined across from one another created an enormously large hallway.

The statues looked down, across and sideways at him. As Bob passed the still figures, he had a sudden urge to turn around.

He felt strongly that he was being watched and studied.

He walked further into the room. A chilling emptiness came at him from nowhere.

Click!

Bob turned his head in the direction of the sound. It started off slowly at first. Bob picking up bits and pieces of words... a melody.The disk.

Phil Collins: 'I Wish It Would Rain' played softly. Bob looked east out of the open French windows.

He always had his way with women. There would always be a lady who had a sense of adventure, who was bored with her life-and with having sex in the same old missionary position with dull unimaginative men. There never seemed to be a shortage of adventurous women who would fly off into the night with him. The mere mention of sensual expression to the furthest reaches of sexual fulfillment was all it took to get them alone.

Ingesting their vital fluids granted him everlasting youth, virility and good looks.

To make the date more interesting, Bob smiled, after he got them alone, relaxed, some good old fashioned hypnosis sealed the entire psychic scenario for his victims.

Bob took off his cape and slung it over one of the four arms of the bronze statue of Shiva Nataraja. It slid off. He kicked off his shoes, his shirt, pants and under-wear. They fell to the floor also.

Bob headed for the shower which was surrounded by ancient pyramid replicas, a statue of King Mycerinus and Queen Khamerernebty and gold coffins. The coffin of Tutankhamen, when the area became steamed, semiprecious stones sparkled like twilight. Amelia loved to sit in the steam the shower made while relaxing in the tub looking up at the gold inlaid coffin.

Bob turned the shower on full blast. The steam escaped immediately covering the twenty foot dressing mirror with its perimeter of clear stage makeup lights.

He walked over and cut the lights on. Bob wiped at what would have been glass and stared at nothing more than gold coffins and pyramids.

It was true, as he smiled, that he did murder some human victims, but it was socially acceptable to solely lust just for the human blood.

Bob stuck out a proud chin agreeing with the women of the night that vampire figures are indeed extremely romantic.

He wiped at the absence of a mirror again, imagining his smooth face, caught up in the thought of himself. His charm over women.The charm that captivated them so he may drain their life so that he may live.

Bob was feeling rather old; tired of the same routine as he stepped into the steaming shower. He yelled and ran out of the shower claiming it was too damn hot patting himself over his shoulders, chest and genitals as he sat on Amelia's bidet.

Searching for comfort, he eyed the handle that turned on the basin like fixture. He never used it before, but in thought, now was as good a time as any, and turned it on.

The water rushed up his buttocks and Bob jumped off the bidet and fell into the sunken Jacuzzi.

Bob emerged from the tubs water shaking the heavy drops from his face. He pulled the band that tied his hair in a tail and loosened it with his fingers until it spread its black laces over his shoulders.

Bob pressed a button and the tub came to life. The bubbles hit at his lower body from several directions, bringing him closer to a tranquil ease.

He reached over to a small wet bar and poured himself a brandy. He swirled the amber brandy in his snifter and drank it down. Bob laid the glass at the edge of the tub as the brandy and the sounds of Bach Fugue washed over him.

Bob rested his head back looking up into the sky light and the exposed wooden beams of the ceiling. With his eyes opened he imagined her there, sitting, standing across from him. He wasn't sure but finally made up his mind to have her sit; cross-legged.

It was a sign to indicate tightness and withdrawal, resistance against anyone reaching them.

Bob leaned up against a wall, watching her with half closed eyes. The insistent look that slips over the surface of a thing and gripped it like a hook. His hips were pushed forward slightly as if they were cantilevered, and his legs apart. He locked his thumbs in his belt right above the pockets with his fingers pointing down towards his privates.

Bob's eyes did far more talking than his body language as they lingered on her throat, breast and body. They lingered sensuously and with intent.

Bob touched his tongue to his lips and narrowed his eyes. Invariably, she became uneasy and excited. She responded to Bob's opening gambit by stroking her hair and rearranging her clothes. Her firm breasts swelled with her breathing, the nipples visible points. She was returning Bob's flattering attention and now she was in too deep to protest.

She spelled out with her movements, "I am frustrated. I am not getting what I need. I am closed in. Let me out. I can be approached and I'm readily available."

She switched her leg from one over the other repeatedly, keeping her thighs close to one another. With one hand, symbolically, open and inviting, affected a gesture and touched her breast in a near caress. Bob ignored this and closed the fantasy.

He picked up a sponge and washed himself clean. It just wouldn't work on Amelia. She'd never fall for such winks and nods he thought.

He jumped out the tub and walked over to a closet and without drying, opened a chest of drawers and slipped on a pair of MickeyMouse underwear and matching socks. He fished around in the closet, pushing clothes aside, sliding them back and forth scrapping the metal hangers against the wooden racks in frustration.

He pulled a purple sweat shirt out with the words Fila Italia in gold letters on its front, and put it on. He stepped into a pair of stone wash jeans and slipped a pair of green, red and black bowling shoes with the number ten stamped to the heels, on his feet. He started to turn away but reached into the dark closet and pulled out a steel blue nylon microfiber trench coat. Bob brushed it and slipped the coat on.

Bob, as he walk past, snatched a hand crafted sterling silver watch from the top of the dresser. He fastened the crocodile strap to his left arm as he walked past the grandfather clock.

Two feet away from the clock Bob stopped, and noticed that his watch had the wrong time. 'But it's a Swiss quartz', he thought and walked back to his dresser.

Bob picked up several other watches from the restored finish dresser. They all had the same time. He eyed his collection curiously and put it on. It was purple, green and red with Mickey's arms curved to the exact time as his designer watch.

Bob walked back in front of the grandfather clock and set the swatch to within the exact second of the clock. With watches on either arm felt strange, but a fashion statement non-the-less.

Bob pulled the double edged crusader from the cape and fastened it inside the trench. He walked past the statues, eyeing each one, and opened the door. A final look inside the apartment, and Bob swore again. "Now for that lunch."

He slammed the door behind him.

***

Doctor Marcus D'Shey was asleep in the soft comforts of the leather wing-back chair. Bridgette was now two hours into the surgery as a black mist etched up the sides of the building entering into every open vent, window and crevices.

A dark altering shadow lingered its way through the draught of the chimney. It melted into the metal gratings roaming over the pepper-fleck carpet.

From underneath a door a milky film, oddly shaped as the first, spread over the doctor's legs and hips, stopping at his shoulders.

"Wake up," A voice said. "wake up doctor, wake up."

A dozen hours seemed to tick away; the measurements of silence, as the doctor was viciously slapped.

Marcus shook his head, recalling the sting of a dream and looked up into the bare gray eyes of Bob.

He blinked frantically wiping at the corners

of his eyes with his hands.

"What do you want? How did you get in here?" The doctor said, looking nervously around.

"Information, the chimney, elevator shaft and cooling vents." Bob said. "I'm ready for the lightening round now."

"You're an uninvited guest, so get out now before I call security." Marcus said, still looking nervously around the apartment.

"Well can I at least buy a vowel Pat?"

"A what." Marcus questioned.

"Relax little fellah." Bob sat on the edge of the desk, reached down and grabbed the doctor's knee. "Just relax. It will all be over soon and quite painless."

"You're here to kill me," Marcus stated.

"aren't you?"

"No, no, no... get a grip will ya'. You're making me nervous."

Bob got up.

"You've been hounding me for years with that wooden stick and I can't quite figure out why." Bob said.

Bob turned his back on Marcus. The Doctor reached for something on a long table behind him against the wall. On the table was an electrical apparatus with colored lights above it, two pistol grip epees hung on the wall which were wired to the machine. On the same table sat storage racks filled with information disks.

Bob turned around and Marcus jerked his arm back, luckily, without Bob noticing.

"A steak through the heart would kill me

probably, and just as quickly as eating something that was bad for me, like toxic waste." Bob said.

The Doctor's eyes narrowed.

"I guess you're wondering which one will do the trick." Bob said.

"No," Marcus replied nervously. "not really."

"Well, you do want something. And I need information. You scratch my back, and I'll scratch yours. Just like old times." Bob joked.

"We have no old times." Marcus said courageously, leaning slightly forward in the wing back.

"Don't get testicle on me," Bob said shoving an open hand in the doctor's face. "let's be friends."

Marcus looked down at the open hand and slowly reached for it. Midway through accepting his offer, he drew his arm back and looked up at Bob. Marcus turned his attention to the table, now beside him, and moved his hand slowly outward towards it. Bob slipped his hand inside the left side of the blue trench and studied the table and the area around it. Marcus looked up at Bob as if to say, 'Is it okay?' In silence, Bob gave his approval watching Marcus closely.

"I'm desperate." Bob said as he clutched the handle of the double-edge crusader inside his coat.

Marcus solemnly reached for the storage rack marked 'D' chapter. He ran his finger up the side, stopped and pulled out a disk.

Marcus swiveled in the leather chair. It squealed with a whine as Marcus was now facing a dozen terminals. The one to his far left ticked away at the seconds of Bridgette's awakening. At his far right, where Bob stood, was a separate computer with its own tower hardware. All but the one linked to Bridgette were down.

Marcus tapped the desk looking from the corner of his eye and asked Bob what was his problem hoping he'd move away from the computer next to him.

"I'm in love Doc."

"That's it." Marcus said.

"There's more to it. It's damn right confusing and I need your help Doc."

Bob walked away from the computer and turned his back, but quickly faced Marcus again.

With a keystroke the half table turned and

the desired computer was now placed in front of Marcus. He booted the system and laid the disk next to the tower.

"Well," Marcus said with a sigh. "how can I help?"

Bob felt relaxed and so did Marcus who leaned back and folded his arms behind his head.

"I'm in love."

"You said that."

"Well isn't that enough."

"No," Marcus said. "why don't you tell me a little bit more about her and why you think it's a problem."

Marcus leaned over and inserted the disk. With several keystrokes, he loaded the program, and sat back again.

"Well, she has eyes you can drown in, mysterious; captivating liquid pools like an endless sea. Her smile, laugh and words wash over you, almost hypnotic. And her touch. How can I say this without sounding too corny Doc."

Marcus leaned over, relaxed and interested.

"Please," Marcus said. "continue."

"She touches you as if she cares... no, healing you from inside. And she touches me a lot. I ought to know." Bob said as he moved his jaw from side to side.

Bob feeling comfortable with the conversation turned his back to Marcus.

Marcus quietly got up and tipped-toed to the table and switched the electrical apparatus on. He reached for the epee and noticed his hand trembling. Marcus looked over to the computer terminal. The digital readings ticked backwards were of no help as his arm continued to shake. He slid the epee from the hooks. Bob's back was still turned; a mild, almost childlike voice lingered in an even tone.

"... and her body spills sexuality. And the way she waaaaa..."

Bob squealed, which sounded more like a puppies yelp. His eyes sprang open and he held up his arms as if he were being robbed and looked around as much as he could without moving his head.

"Either I've been stabbed," Bob said. "or goosed. You're in big trouble fellah if I turn around and find you sniffing your finger."

Bob turned around. "Ah, swordplay."

He drew his crusader from the catch inside

the blue trench.

"En grade." Bob said happily.

Marcus jumped back, leveling the pistol-grip epee throwing out a warning shout.

"No, no wait." Marcus said cautiously. "This is no weapon. It's to get," he swallowed. "a sample of your DNA."

Bob lowered the sword and tilted his head slightly left. Marcus jumped back again.

"Deoxyribo Nucleic Acid." Bob said, pronouncing each word clearly.

Marcus leaned his head to the right. "You know about that?"

"It's the main constituent of the chromosomes of living cells, consisting of two long chains of phosphate and sugar units twisted into a double helix and joined by hydrogen bonds in a sequence that determines individual heredity characteristics.... How am I doing?" Bob said gleefully.

Marcus stared. He shook his head trying to remember what had happened.

"Fine, you're doing just fine."

Marcus looked down to the terminal. The configurations and data were running wild. He dropped the epee and sat down. Marcus typed in several commands and a red light in the tower began to blink. It was recording the information to the disk.

"So, what's it saying about me?" Bob asked.

"Well it's saying... I don't know, I'd have to study it."

"Can I look?" Bob asked.

"Yeah, be my guest."

Bob placed a hand on the table and leaned close to the computer. Marcus just looked at him; studying.

"You're recording this aren't you Doc?"

"Yes." Marcus said nervously. "I can stop it if you want."

"Well since you obviously have what you want," Bob looked at Marcus. "now maybe we can continue with my problem."

"Yes, by all means." Marcus said.

"Okay." Bob placed the sword back into the trench, clasped his hands together and looked up towards the ceiling. "You have tire marks on your ceiling."

Marcus looked up and smiled. Bridgette had been riding along side the wooden beams across the ceiling. No wonder he couldn't spot her. He knew Bridgette couldn't hear that but looked inside the windows, then down at the clock. It was still counting backwards.

"So," Bob clapped his hands together making Marcus jump again. "she tells me to stop fighting her. I've never hit her. Then she says to be myself. Who else can I be? And then she says being apart sometimes is healthy. Healthy for whom, me or her? And then she leaves. Says she's with friends. And has sex with a toy when I'm damn willing, able, healthy and strong. And last but not least... trust me. Sometimes I don't trust that but who else can I trust? All her eggs are not in my basket and I get real hungry some times. You follow me so far Doc?"

"I guess so."

"Well you had to be there." Bob said.

"I guess you need some romance in your life." Marcus said and couldn't believe he said it.

"Romance, I'm the most romantic guy on this planet. I'm a vampire remember. Women fall to their knees at some of the crap I come up with Doc."

"But-" Marcus uttered.

"Look at these eyes." Bob continued. "The lids compressed the look and shoot out like an arrow. It's the look I've studied on and mastered for centuries. The look as if asleep but which behind the cloud of sweet drowsiness are utterly awake."

"Bedroom eyes I've heard them called." Marcus interrupted.

"And anyone who has such a look

possesses a treasure." Bob said.

He looked as if he were about to cry and Marcus felt for him, then stopped.

"Yeah," Marcus cleared his throat. "if I may make an observation."

"It's about time Doc."

"Love is like a satellite out there circling our Earth for some four billion years like a beautiful but lonesome paradise trying to catch a lover's eye. It's regarded as the mansion of the fathers, the residence of the souls of those who have passed away and are there waiting to return to rebirth. As we see it, it dies and is resurrected and we watch, stargazed. And if we wrap our arms around it and search out its wonders and mysteries, we are learning simultaneously the wonders of ourselves. A moon flight as an outward journey is outward into us." Marcus highlighted.

Bob just stared; stony face.

"Yeah, so what's your point?" Bob asked.

Marcus leaned back in the leather chair.

"Take her to the moon." Marcus said.

Silence.

"That's beautiful. A trip to the moon. Amelia would love that Doc."

Marcus eyes bulged.

"I know you don't mean that physically," Bob said. "but it's all becoming clear to me now."

"What was that name again?" Marcus asked. "The woman you just mentioned."

"Who, Amelia?"

"Yes, yes. And her last name. What's her last name?" Marcus asked excitedly.

"I don't know." Bob said. "I never thought to ask. Anyway, who cares? I have a new lease on life now Doc. You're looking at one happy camper."

Bob twirled around. Spinning and spinning to a song: "Looking for love in all the wrong places, looking for love in too many faces, I'm looking ... I'm looking for love..."

Marcus took out the disk and placed it next to the tower. He leaned over, ran his finger up then down a storage rack and pulled out another disk. He inserted it and loaded the program.

Marcus looked over into the operating room. It was a white midnight inside; nothing visible. The digital clock left three hours and forty minutes until Bridgette's awakening.

The readings of the ectoplasmicparticles happened four times at different intervals and different places.

Marcus wanted to match the particles up to see if they coincided but it would take too long. At this point, he could possibly kill two birds with one stone... maybe three.

He looked at the clock again, then back to the terminal. A complete dossier on Amelia jumped out at him. With a keystroke, he read as the file rolled up like an ancient scroll.

He needed more information. If Bridgette were there, complete charts, records and digital information would be available in seconds but at this pace it would take hours to read and collect it all. But he had to be sure. He could get what he needed from the source. There could be thousands of Amelia's and his Amelia might be one of them. So why not ask. He thought.

"So where did you two crazy kids meet?"

Marcus asked as he looked up at Bob.

Bob stopped spinning and looked curiously at Marcus.

"Germany." Bob answered.

With one hand, Marcus punched up origin of birth. It immediately responded and a place in Germany was confirmed. But not good enough. Marcus needed more.

"You guys been together long?"

"As quiet as it's kept," Bob said. "I'd be giving away her beauty secrets. But since it's you, and we're tight like that," Bob crossed his fingers. "I'll tell you. Oh, I'd say about, uh close to one-thousand years, give or take."

Marcus eyes bulged. He looked at the screen, then back at Bob. He started to sweat and tremble.

"And uh," Marcus cleared his throat. "you still don't know her last name?"

"What's in a name? A rose by any other name would smell just as sweet. What are you putting into that machine? And why such a fuss over my Amelia, Doc."

Bob drew his sword and it was placed immediately at the doctor's throat.

Bob read what was on the screen. Marcus held his breath feeling the dizziness of possibly passing out.

"What is this? Why do you have this information on Amelia? Where did you get it? Speak up. You don't have to answer them all in that order. Talk damn it!"

Marcus pointed at the tip of the sword which was placed neatly at his cervical.

"Oh, sorry." Bob said and pulled the sword

away.

Marcus exhaled and clutched his throat. He swallowed deeply and touched his tongue to his lips.

"We're in grave danger and you may be able to stop it." Marcus said.

"What danger? What are you talking about Doc?"

"666, the number of the beast."

"The what Doc?"

"The figure of the Anti-Christ." Marcus swallowed again. "He will be born again in flesh."

"Yeah, so." Bob flinched.

Marcus continued. "All genuine occult tradition points to a year. When the second multiple of 666 occurred in history in AD

1332, the sun demon Sorath, the third of the trinity of evil inspired the torture and the burning of the leading knights by working through their possessed souls. The very spirit of materialism will incarnate in the flesh personally to direct the total destruction of the spiritual aims of mankind. The following thirty years of the twenty-first century we'll see the war between good and evil in the battle for the Earth. And in the third decade of the next century a tremendous sequence of apocalyptic events will begin."

"So what does this have to do with me?" Bob asked.

"Listen," Marcus stood up. "there has already been two great planetary alignments in the last two decades, but that alignment which is close to the earthly alignment of planetary sites will happen soon. That will be the date of the critical turning point of the apocalypse."

Bob threw his hands up.

"I still don't follow you." Bob said.

Marcus became frantic and began to shout and stammer. "1998. That's the year he was expected to be born but it is his character to act unpredictably. He must be stopped. He must be killed. And you can do it."

"So what does this have to do with Amelia?" Bob asked.

"She's working with him in the destruction of man. She must either be possessed," Marcus swallowed again but this time there was a dry response. He was almost unable to continue, but managed to put the last remaining words together. "or killed."

Marcus studied Bob. He seemed to be taking the news better than he suspected. He exhaled again and tried to relax without hyperventilating.

"Oh and how do you plan to do that? Is that information on those circles you put in there?" Bob asked.

"By saying her first and last name to her face. One, it would hold her bound to the one who pronounces it correctly or two, it will kill her." Marcus said cautiously.

"How can a name do that to a vampire? I say her name all the time. You're stupid." Bob laughed.

"You've never joined the two names and she's no vampire. She's a witch." Marcus said as a matter of fact.

Bob put the sword back up to the doctor's throat. Marcus leaned back as much as he could balance himself on the heels of his shoes.

"I've killed many men who have uttered those words sir. She is no witch. Give me that circle or die." Bob demanded coldly.

"There it is," Marcus managed to say. "take it, it's yours."

Bob took the disk from the table and put it in the inside pocket of the blue trench. He raised the sword high in the air and sliced the computer in two pieces.

Bob placed the sword back up to the doctor's throat.

"And this name," Bob said. "what is it?"

"Auer, Amelia Auer. Say those two names together and it will do exactly as I've said."

"If I ever see you around Amelia, I'll kill you." Bob threatened.

Bob spun on his heels and walked towards the window. Marcus turned around and looked at the digital clock. He took in a deep breath and stared at Bob's back. Bob was carving the stripping from around the tinted windows. Marcus flipped the epee up into his hand with the tip of his shoe.

"I'm not afraid to die." Marcus said.

"So be it." Bob replied.

Bob turned on Marcus with the sword leveled. Marcus was bouncing up and down mumbling to himself.

"Keep well balanced, crouch the body, knees bent, weapon out in front of the middle of the body, arm bent, and weapon slightly above the wrist." Marcus mumbled.

Bob watched Marcus as he counted to himself.

"What are you doing?" Bob asked.

"... three!"

Marcus lunged in Bob's direction. He countered the move as the blades met and stepped aside. The duel lasted for two minutes as Bob stabbed the doctor in the chest.

Marcus stammered back which took great effort. His arms and legs felt as if they were full of lead and the air ran out of oxygen. He fell into the wing-back chair holding his chest and dropped the epee. He thought he might be having a heart attack and tried to remember what to do, how to help himself. He looked down at his chest. The blood pushed out between his fingers. He took one final look at Bob.

"Beware of the spear of Longinus." Marcus said between breaths.

Bob stepped closer.

"It has two parts and is held in place by gold, silver and copper threads and a silver sheath. If you meet him, he will have this." Marcus coughed up blood.

"Who?" Bob asked. "Meet who?"

Marcus just stared. He was dead.

Bob closed the lids of the doctor's eyes and walked away. He turned again sharply. Two small yellow lights held close together shined from within the glass room behind Marcus. Bob dismissed it as no threat as he sensed no one else was present. He turned and headed for the window. Bob pushed the pain out into the street, put one leg over the edge of the window and looked back. The lights were gone and Bob, concentrating on darkness, melted into a shadow and disappeared.

***

Amelia was now at the edge of the free world. A small cloud, growing as it approached her carried with it a strange call. The cloud began to spread and seemed to be traveling at the speed of a crawl. She could hear the call now as the cloud covered the sky. It was laugher. A high pitched laugher. The cloud swept through her as the wraith-like form of Amelia floated above the Atlantic Ocean.

The various sounds chopped at the wind.

Poems, sonnets, movie titles flashed before her eyes. No, it was her life she saw.

The Caribbean shipwreck in 1798. The New York dock fire in 1835. The Chicago fire, 1871.

The cloud continued its dramatic intercourse with her past. Amelia wanted to rise above it, dive beneath... zap it to make it go away. Suddenly, it ended in a deformed whine. A shrill so sharp that it could be felt inside her heart. Amelia felt bitter enmity toward its annoyance.

High above the Atlantic, a change, somewhat familiar and strangely resembling the feeling she had inside the cemetery began to boil inside her. A haunting that this would be her last trick on humanity. Maybe even her death.

By means of gnawing the flesh, Amelia was

soon over Ireland. She made a southeastern turn towards Wales. She picked up speed over St. George's Channel rippling the water, forming tiny troughs' of waves on it. For anyone approaching England by air, the first surprise is that 'it really is green.'

Below her was a land that Bob had claimed to have read many books about. Her remembering at this time seemed odd but she smiled as she could hear in the reaches of her mind Bob's voice continually raving on of Shakespeare 'Demi-Paradise' and 'Blessed Plot.' The one that stood out the most was the poet William Blake's 'Green and Pleasant Land.' The land was indeed so pleasantly green.

She could feel the westerly winds ease her strain in flight. Remembering it was also responsible for the variability of the climate...

according to Bob.

To Amelia, she felt that the country had no climate, just weather. And she had first hand at this since Bob never ventured.

Amelia rode the wind down the Thames River. It was out of her way but she thought, 'why not do as the Romans do.' She headed for London.

'At all seasons,' she could hear Bob say as she twist and turned along the rivers banks: 'rain, clouds, and sunlight chase each other across England's skies.' Amelia flew higher to see if she could take back a convincing argument to Bob.

Above the clouds she noticed that a bright, clear sky was no sign of a bright day. Why was she thinking of him. She forced herself to relish the demonic cast of evils the night was to possess. She changed action and dove into the clouds. Amelia could hear the soft splashing of light rain drops as she passed deeper into the thick foliage of clouds.

'Uncertain glory of an April day,' Shakespeare. 'April is the cruelest month,' said the twentieth century T.S. Eliot describing April.

Amelia tried to shake the thoughts and ideas from her mind. Then she heard Bob's voice. "The contemporary Englishman whose umbrella is as necessary as his shoes might agree with both, Amelia."

"But this is October." She said aloud.

Noticing she was in a conversation with herself she covered her ears in denial. She pushed through the clouds and as they rejoined, the deep and far distant roar of thunder could be heard as a lightning bolt shot twenty yards in front of Amelia's face. She closed her eyes and in darkness saw the impression of her history.

The Johnston flood, 1889.Quake and fire, San Francisco, 1906.

The cry of roasting children that he, the Devil loved so much. The last two-hundred years of sacrificing human hearts-blood as she was falling more a victim of the signing of the book. The fear of the book could wait as Amelia's fall from flight was, this day, to end.

Amelia opened her eyes wiping the lids to clear her vision. She gasped as a tall building angled toward her.

'I'm a witch.' She remembered. 'An apparition of my living self.'

She began to feel uneasy over this arrogant spirit of hers and decided to go around it. But she was dazed by the strange daydreams and blinked to ward them off. Her decision to avoid the tall structure was premature as Amelia, solid in body, slammed into the tower.

Majestically dominating the London skyline was Big Ben. And there was now four hands and two legs keeping its time as Amelia lay stamped to its face.

As the Post Office Tower and the Thorn Electric Building stood in their restricted places, Amelia began to slide, hitting the clocks lip tumbling towards Earth. The rush of cool wind awakened her as she faced what seemed to be her end. She closed her eyes, concentrating on a spell. A twenty foot-by forty foot air blown mattress appeared below her. The ones stunt professionals use to break their falls. She relaxed her body letting her spell cheat her from sure death. But as fate would have it, she missed.

A small crowd gathered with one yelling

for the nearest constable.

"Where's a wooden top when you need him?" He asked in the normal glossary of English Briticism.

The woman who stood beside him shrugged her shoulders as if the act was of no great importance. Her face was an accent of old English royalty, stiff lips, double chin, and sagged eyes formed from the battle of prejudices or the weather. But her panic-plum hair which was crinkly and plentiful, and over shaded lips and rouge was the sign of modern English times.

"Probably off having a spot of tea no doubt." Another mimed in a tone of a middle aged crone and not a youthful teenager.

Every observer pulled in a deep breath as Amelia stretched both arms yawning as if she just had her back popped into position. Every move Amelia made, sent the crowd stepping back. She pulled herself out of the hole and faced the confused skeptics.

"Missed it by that much." Amelia said comically holding up the measurements with index finger and thumb.

It appeared that they would never breathe again until she left or handed them an explanation.

She proceeded to walk away. As they made clear passage, a woman in an olive-green leather jacket released the catch to her umbrella holding it securely over her head. It began to rain again and the British woman commented on what a bit of a berk she was. She had a sharp British accent. It was a strange thing about that language that one could measure the class by the tones. She was a three. Its meaning held no interest to

Amelia but the light laughter did. Amelia looked over her shoulder and keeping in step stared into her eyes. Amelia flicked her fingers in the woman's direction. The woman began to feel a pain in her stomach followed by a severe aching as if she had to relieve herself. All eyes turned in the woman's direction and in her embarrassment wanted to move quickly as the feeling of urination was unstoppable. She padded herself with one hand, then both. A liquid pushed out between her fingers then ran the length of her tight blue knickers. She examined the flow separating both hands, then in a panic, locked her knees together. The stench was as pungent as a five day old corpse that lie baking in the sun. Her hands were cerise in color and her stomach pushed the resin from her body covering her legs and feet with a yellowish-purple afterbirth secretion. She looked around for help. Each breath not allowing a single word to be spoken until it pushed the liquid from her body. Everyone had left, and so did Amelia, leaving the woman in a pool of her own fluids. A moment later she was back to her normal self as it were, and then she fainted.

Amelia took another look at the clock tower. She stared through myopic black eyes. The face of the clock was cracked now and the bells that sounded the hours and quarters were ringing in her ears.

Her view became up-surged with pictures of a holocaustic fire that raged through central London in the nineteenth century crumbling the palace of Westminster. All that remained was a section of 1526 Cloister and the medieval Westminster Hall.

The tower sat at its eastern end, and scenes of a new palace and the light of beauty brought her back from what was becoming a nervous breakdown. She felt something was wrong. Her travel was perfect. She passed the stars coming close to the moon. It was viewed in terms of the rhythmic life of the cosmos governing all vital change; her change. Not the twenty-eight days of mortal women but the all too known twenty-nine. The new moon.An evil period necessitating strict taboos against beginning any new or creative period.The period to her, the coming of the five.As a male form, particularly in regards to Amelia, was understood that this evil would come at each full moon to take her. From the land of the dead, the place to which souls ascend after death, an evil and dangerous figure would appear in one or all of its five names. How she dreaded this life; this change; this lunar governance of a cycle likewise leading to sexual intercourse in association of the moon and her fate. She was to be at the Sabbath and could hear the drums pounding in her heart. Lucifer calling out to her. The music making her sway and dizzy, but never taking over her tenacious will. It was too odd a feeling and Amelia felt the urge not to resist. But the nightmare of her past circled her head and she put both hands to her ears to silence the screams.

The lust of the Devil and the five evils sent to seduce her racked her body in mist like form. She discharged a sexual ooze that soaked the pouch of her laced-leaf garment. Again the calling of the flesh weakened her as she stood massaging her secret part. She had to go to him. The flesh that satisfied her and brought her to a fit of ecstasy. She jerked her head up to the sky and with her arms straining downwards towards the earth; she screamed.

Amelia walked aimlessly through the streets of central London, trying desperately to sort out her world.

She passed the medieval gothic church of St. Margaret's, a placid precinct on the edge of Victoria Street. Then through the old memories of the slums of 1851 to Victoria Station. The aged and the modern scenes twirled around her head like an venerable marry-go-round. Much of the bold Victorian architecture along the street was styled in indifferent contemporary, including a twenty-two story glass box, the Westminster City Hall.

Her walk became more pleasant now as she continued up Downing Street westward towards Buckingham Palace. She marveled at the sites completely forgetting about time and its importance.

St. James Palace was just a site away as she walked into the oldest ornamental of the six central royal parks. St. James Park gave the west end of London a heritage of beauty, repose, and sense of continuity. The Whitehall building, topped with pinnacles and towers formed a silent Arabian nights silhouette. The weeping willows swaying to an unseen breeze around the lake added an oriental touch to an extremely artful landscape.

She brushed happily past the flower beds lifting her legs high in a walk as if skipping.

Pelicans in a sleepy squat along the lake gave the park a splendid ceremonial atmosphere that terminated all Amelia's fears.

Amelia bent to grasp a dying flower with the gentle touch of a woman in love. She inhaled softly and the forty-thousand tulips and fourteen-thousand geraniums that shape the English landscape came immediately to life. Amelia giggled with delight. But her praise to a blossoming evening was shorten by the mark of the Druids placed high above St. James Palace walls.

The shocking crime of the 1971 Los Angeles earthquake and hurricane Hugo passed before her eyes. The disastrous years were catching up with her. Amelia's cheeks filled out and her eyes started to swell. Her first thought was to run away... and she did. Amelia ran through the flower beds crushing the precious peddles beneath her feet. Her pace quickened as the memories kept its nightmarish attacks. Amelia ran towards the bulky Queen Victoria Memorial putting as much distance between her and her sordid history as she possibly could.

Once outside the park Amelia stood listening closely to an enemy; her nemesis. So devious, so shrewd in this method of attack. His strategy was endless and surprising. He missed no opportunity for destructive intervention into her affairs. His advantage was to be invisible. His efforts cloaked by stealth and subterfuge served to characterize both his ends and his means. The Prince of darkness was summoning her to worship with him. She aimed at an end to his chastising and walked around to the Palace gate. The monarch was not in residence as this was October. The royal standard wasn't flying from the roof but the guard was in the forecourt which is changed every morning the rest of the year whetherof not the monarch is in residence.

She positioned herself in front of the palace guard who stood with a gravely solid attitude. Amelia, without purpose or reason entered his mind. Once inside she toyed with his fears and fantasies. He was indeed short on fears and long on fantasies.

In order to put the calling to rest, she called upon Loa. And if her act proved worthy, if she pleased his sexual appetite, they would indeed delay their taunting and it would be quite possible to pursue an objective course. She put her plan to work.

A sadistic scene ensued inside the palace guards head yet he assumed a natural pose.

Amelia walked up to him wearing a lovely black peignoir. Her hair was spilled across her shoulders.

"Well, hello." He said in a tone of a man in control and not a stuffy warder. It threw Amelia for a loop, his sudden command of speech. It interested her. He had large warm eyes and his nose was large but not too obtrusive. All she could do or wanted to do was to see what would happen next. Her wait was short.

"You seem to have the ability of being alone. That means you trust yourself and so I figured I can trust you too." The yeoman said.

"And how do you know that? I don't even know you." Amelia said trying to pull the conversation her way. He got up and walked towards her with gentle, disingenuous air.

"Your nightgown... your hair. You're not one for games." He said. "If so, maybe there's something we can play."

Amelia became uneasy; nervous. She also noticed that he had nothing on. Was this her fantasy or his.

"You're no good at trying to be adamant."

He stated calmly.

Amelia leaned back.

"There's a right time and place for everything and you've definitely come at the right time." He told Amelia as he reached for her. Amelia stepped back, and he stepped closer... in breaths reach.

"Your imagination has gotten the better of you." Amelia said. "This is not what..."

His motions got the better of her. He was tall and friendly but possessing the kind of angular face that could turn mean suddenly. She stumbled from his closeness but caught herself by the edge of something behind her.

"I imagine our day of expensive foreplay, with you, after your bath, stretching out on the veranda like a young cat savoring the sun wasn't your idea of telling me that maybe, just maybe, I had a chance." He said blandly.

"I'm sorry," Amelia said nervously. "I don't remember any of that."

He was close enough now where she could feel an intense passion from his body. In her confusion of how he could do this was inviting and she welcomed it.

He was gentle as he touched her; kissed her. Amelia reached behind his head pulling him closer, their lips and tongue in an epic enclosure of physical lust. With both hands on the straps of her gown he tore the peignoir from her body. She was shocked and a little frightened. The kind of excitement that made her blood rush through her body keeping her alive and her body liquefied.

He pushed her back on a black teak desk spinning her so her head fell over its edge and below his privates. She covered her breast and drew in her lips. He stepped closer and sodomized her orally. When he was done he lifted her off the desk. Amelia pushed him away and he slapped her. It was unexpected and the blow dazed her. He shoved her and Amelia's head fell into the softness of satin pillows. The dream was diffused, as if another person had inhabited the body whose legs spread open, welcoming and willing as he gave and took the amazing pleasure he felt was his to give and take.

The guards and her own urgencies had tangled her hair, both moving her head this way and that way, in and out of the soft square feathered pillows.

He sodomized her objectively, sitting her upon his lap groping her savagely between her legs. He threw her to the floor. A sign of sadistic cruelty that only Lucifer and his demons could love.

Amelia looked up from her kneeling position. His strength arched limp to the floor. She roughly grabbed him by the sack of his privates and pulled him across the floor. He kicked and screamed as gently as he could without tempting their removal.

Amelia stepped from the dream... spent.

The palace guards' expression never changed. Amelia was dumbfounded, shaking her head in disbelief. She walked up to him with a look of a woman scorned, grabbed him by the privates and cut them off.

A hundred expressions fluttered across his face.

"Trick or treat." She said amusingly as she held out her hands and in them; nothing.

He stepped back blinking and wetting his

lips with his tongue. "You wanton woman. You filthy scarlet."

He fumbled for the rifle pulling the flintlock back trying to make it catch. Amelia, again the object of confusion, searched her thoughts not knowing what to do, or what course to take. Her head pounding. Her body aching.

'Run!' It was a refreshing thought and a wise suggestion as the flintlock became stationed in its firing position.

Amelia pulled her silk woven gown up to her knees. She ran in place. Her legs picking up speed until they became a mere blur. The palace guard took aim but it was too late. Amelia took off like a shot in the dark. The palace guard fired. Her speed was not like that of the revolutions per minute the bullet shared with the wind, but close enough so the two raced as though they were in the hundred yard dash. The single bullet reaching for her and Amelia pulling away. At one point the copper pellet passed her and Amelia, too vain to realize, ran faster. She pushed herself over the greenbelt's of central London past roads, through the towns of Bristol, cities of Wales until she was over the North Atlantic Ocean beating the sting of the palace guards rage by outnumbered kilometers. Now heading home, she was euphoric but wondering what in the world to do next.

Amelia stopped in the middle of the Atlantic, her body hovering two feet above water and looked back at the small island of England. She wiped her forehead bringing a hand across her face to her cheek. Black make-up stained her arms and fingers. She thought to herself. 'That never happened before.' And dropped into the ocean.

6

Heart-pounding drums, and ear piercing tambourines covered with human hides herald the coming of the thirteenth hour.

The key to addict the listener, a flute and words to every song or melody were used this night as a form of hypnotism, as bare chest women gathering twist in a crazy feverish dance around a bonfire. The men slashing themselves on their chests and wrist with knives. Blood, sweat, and rain tangled in shiny rivulets over their dark skins.

Spices, incense and body orders mingle in a hazy theatrical fog, as three figures, sprawl and grunt in the extremities of the shadows.

One woman lies panting, pitching herself forward repeatedly on her face with her buttocks high in the air as another pushes a large devise deep inside her.

Men and women in ecstasy stomp and howl in a circle as the rain began to slack and clouds part. Suddenly, a woman throws up her arms, snatches a hunting knife from the ground and cuts off her left breast. She throws it into the fire. The flames leap and spray the night with sparks. She falls to one knee as several men take privilege with her in every orifice.   Afterwards, they sacrifice her and throw her dead body into the fire.

Round and round they dance around the flames, ocher and blood gleaming in the firelight, symbols and chains jiggle and spin. Raw palms beat out the mood; shinning chest heave and breast shiver in the shadows with the throbbing feelings in their phallus they thrust into unforgivable sin.

Spurting vitality across a glistening pair of large, honey-brown breast, a humble servant shakes then cries out as much from pleasure as from knowing that his prayers will be transmitted without haste to the spirits of the afterlife.

The rain turned to soft drizzle, and then was gone.   The dark low clouds left and headed southwest towards America.   Shortly before the clouds scheduled departure over the horizon, the moon suddenly emerged for a brief appearance. It was a glorious sight to behold as the most evil people living in the horrible darkness, the Druid priest, demanded another human blood sacrifice.

These men of oak, the Druid priest, were so filled with demons that some had strange frightening powers. People lived in terror of the Druids.

On Halloween the Druids and their followers went from castle to castle playing trick or treat. The treat from the castle demanded by Druids would be a princess or some woman for human sacrifice. If the treat pleased the Druids... they would leave a Jack O' Lantern with a lighted candle made of human fat to protect those inside from being killed by demons that night. When some unfortunate couldn't meet the demands of the

Druids, then it was time for the trick.

A hexagram was drawn on the front door of Warwick Castle. That night Satan's demons spilled through the keyholes of the 14th century fort taking refuge inside the 17th century mansion. The castle overlooking the Avon River gave it a mystical knights of the round table appearance. They would kill someone or everyone through fear meeting the demands of the ceremony. Through their dreams, the people, servants or keepers of the land were subjected to unfortunate accidents.

Jessica didn't sleep that night staying up to do some last minute cleaning in the kitchen. She washed the ten foot long butcher block table humming a natural tune of "CalonLan." The powerful wave of the lyric gave insight into the nature if her Welsh heart.

She wore a white robe with nothing underneath and as she walked, the spilt fell aside exposing a fleshy thigh. Jessica was not attractive but stunning in a natural sense. Her short blond hair, blue eyes, and button nose was her appealing features. Her large breast pushed out against the terri-cloth. Even more so as the robe was bound tightly by the waist.

A nipple showed and a soft breeze brushed against it. She pulled the cotton fabric over her chest searching for an unexpected onlooker and found none. She continued to clean, bending over now and then revealing her sexiness slightly. Wanting to be noticed but knowing that no one was there. A fantasy held close to her. A secret she dare tell no one, as the corner of the table, as she reached for the middle trying to erase a spot there, alerted a tender area between her legs. She tinged slightly pulling her arm back to see if anyone was watching.

She reached out to the spot on the table again and parted her legs easing up on the corner of the table. It touched her again sending erotic signals throughout her body. The demons watched as she moved her hips in small circles. Both arms stretched out along the table as she climbed on top. The moment and feeling passed as she laid staring up into the ceiling. She touched and rubbed her body but it wasn't the same as before. She laid another minute wanting the feeling to strike her again.

She eyed the sink with its rows of knives resting in their blocks and other kitchen utensils hanging, sitting, and stationed neatly in rows of containers with the handles held outward for easy withdraw. Her eyes fantasized on a rolling pin then to a meat tenderizer. They were both made of wood with thick smooth cylinders. She could easily except them into herself she thought, but the mood would deteriorate as soon as she got up to reach for them. She eyed them suspiciously as she spread her legs. Her breathing became a challenge. Her heart pounded and her buttocks stiffened as Jessica closed her eyes.

The rolling pin was pulled from its resting place, but she didn't hear its removal. It was pushed tenderly into her and the confusion was only brief as she, in thought, assumed it to be her imagination; the climax of her fantasy. She opened her legs further inviting what she thought was all in her head.

At her peak, in almost a feverish pitch, the rolling pin was pushed, to the small rolling handle, deep inside her. Jessica's body arched. Her mouth and eyes opened to almost tearing at the ends as the demons snatched her off the table.

The spell binding beat of the Druids music filled the night as the ceremony continued. The men assaulted Jessica and they brutally sacrificed her to the Gods of many names, the horned hunter of the night, the oak God of the underworld-Satan.

The Druid priest carried long staffs with the ANKH symbol on the high tip. Their religion was thought to be outlawed around 98-180 AD. But they went underground and were secretly active since.

The Druids were so powerful, under their control; the picts would deliberately jump on a

Roman spear so the pict behind him could kill the Roman soldier. The captured Roman soldiers would be burned alive in cages over barren ground. The Druids would call fourth Elfin fire out of the Earth to consume the victims... and it would.

Their night was Halloween. In the occult it is called "Samhain" October 31st. Stonehenge, in England, is the temple site for many of the occult murders. And tonight, as he sat high on his throne savoring the torture, indiscriminate intercourse and slaughtering, he would soon rise in flesh.

The Druid high priest summoned for another human sacrifice.

A cloaked shadow stood wearing a black double crepe coat with a hooded caplet vest and black boots. The same as the Druid priest. It walked over to the fire and pulled the hood from its face. It was Meribeth.

She disrobed and the Devil in seeing her body yelled for the Earth to stop and it appeared that it did. Satan walked from his throne sheepishly standing in back of Meribeth. He turned her around. Satan was ten feet tall with the moon back-lighting his head. Meribeth obeyed soberly as the Devil picked at her face pulling her right eye from its socket. He threw it into the fire and it sizzled.

"Can I return with you?" Meribeth asked.

"Yes," said Satan. "if you would be willing to walk with me across the rubble of the world on bare feet."

Satan spread his arms wide and held his head up laughing into the night. The composed series of holes, stones, and archways that were arranged mostly in circles, with the inner twenty-nine to thirty marked positions were counted off in silence as Meribeth was pushed towards the alter stone. The Druid high priest raised his staff above the silence. The chant for the Elfin fire began.

In the largely treeless tract, the cries of "O mighty Kernos," could be heard throughout the three-hundred square miles of Salisbury Plain. As there were no Roman soldiers or slaves to be found, the Druids caged thirteen soldiers from a nearby army camp in Tidworth over solid ground.

Lucifer sat back in his stone chair as the Earth opened up emitting pitted flames. The screams and cries for mercy were like a delicious melody to Satan as he moved to the rhythm breathing smoke from his mouth and nostrils. The flames reached higher until a roar like thunder shook everyone off their feet.

"STOP!"

The heat from his breath fueled the formation of a cauliflower-like cumulus cloud. If it reached its full peak would blossom into another down pour covering the moon completely.

Again Satan spoke. "Where's Amelia?"

***

Amelia walked through the open French windows and they closed behind her. With her head bowed she walked up to the coffee table and pushed it aside. Amelia knelt pulling the carpet away from the hole and lifted the soiled rag from its grave. She closed her eyes and rubbed her chest. The silk garment she wore melted from her body.

Amelia walked through their cathedral apartment weighing the flesh in her hand. She stopped at the southeast wall and looked up into the 18th century painting by Goya: Witches Lamp.

She unfolded the rag and the pungent order of the serpents tongue pierced her sensitive nose. She put the flesh to her face and rubbed it against her lips. It stiffened immediately. With one hand Amelia leaned against the wall under the painting. She took the stiff tongue and slipped it her partially spread legs. The warmth from the ridged tongue mingled with the juices of her own body. Her thighs stroked the serpents tongue as she glided it up against her secret part. She touched her tongue to her lips and looked down between her legs. The sight brought on other fantasies as she inserted the flesh to its fullest inside of her.

Click.

Amelia jerked the serpents tongue away from her body. The act proved to be positive as thousands of needles picked at her toes, back of her knees, curve of her lower buttocks, arch of her back, and the nape of her neck making her eyes slam shut from sheer eroticism. She grunted as if it hurt.

Amelia screwed her head from left to right trying to put her lust aside. She held her breath and angled her head from side to side filtering through the quiet. Amelia exhaled. It was the disk. Roxettes: 'Listen to your heart' played evenly throughout the masonry construction of the room.

She was attracted to the song looking down at the stiff serpents tongue feeling cheep and useless. But the pains came again. A sour taste sat on the back of her throat as if she would soon throw up. She snapped her fingers and the song stopped. Amelia threw her arm length wise, out towards the closet. With her fingers arched, a black cashmere slip-dress and matching cardigan floated into her hand. She gracefully slipped it on and wrapped the cape around her shoulders. A pair of suede boots walked towards her. She stepped into them and they laced themselves.

The pain came again, just barely as Amelia steadied herself on Bob's lazy-boy recliner. It rocked and Amelia fell to the floor. She picked herself up breathing heavily through her nose. Amelia straightened her body and took in a deep breath. She exhaled slowly feeling the flesh wiggle inside her hand. Amelia held the serpents tongue out in front of her and slowly eased it into her mouth sucking and licking at its wrinkles. Her nipples raised and rubbed up against the cashmere fabric as her breathing became strong heaves. She grabbed and pulled at its points letting the cape fall from her shoulders. Amelia withdrew the tongue and ran over to a half circular sofa that sat in front of a fireplace. She hissed and the logs ignited.

Amelia lay back, and raised the slip-dress to her waist. The pain came again. Sharp stabbing agonizing misery.

Click.

Her throat was dry and her stomach tied up in cramps. She looked over the edge of the sofa at the CD player. No LED lights, not another sound... nothing.

Amelia managed a faithful stand and walked past a statue she didn't recognize and stopped.

'It's him.' She thought.

The laughter started. First inside her head then it burst out into the room. The apartment seemed to spin in dizzying cycles until they became face to face. He stood twelve feet high in his boldness. Rippling flesh, piercing eyes and an unearthly sneer.

"Isn't there something you forgot to do today?" He said in a baritone voice.

Amelia was accustomed to wallow in madness, feigning all laughter... denying all tears. Tears of sorrow, anger, or joy.

She looked down at the flesh, then up at him. The flesh, him. Her teeth were clenched together and her eyes slanted in demonic frustration.

"Look, I just want to do it." Amelia lashed out. "Either strap this son-of-a-bitch on or get the hell out."

"Sign the book."

"Get real." Amelia huffed.

"There is only one reality," Lucifer said. "the reality of your sense of worth."

"I've served you faithfully. The eruption of Mount St. Helens, the earthquakes in Greece, Nicaragua, Turkey and Mexico City." Amelia began to stutter as the pain came back. "dedededede earthquake in Soviet Armenia which alone had a death toll of over one-hundred thousand. The flood in the Sudan, in Bangladesh and the Punjab. Drought and famine in Africa, freak weather conditions in the United States like Hurricane Gilbert. It destroyed vast tracts in the Caribbean, central America and parts of the United States. And the AIDS epidemic. They went apes when they couldn't find a cure." Amelia said feeling faint.

"Have you not perceived the coming catastrophes Amelia? Or are you still clinging to that fixation of love?" Lucifer asked as he wiped the mucus from his nostrils with his twisted fingers.

"Love?" Amelia said simply.

"I will see to it that the individual human spirit will be abolished. Man will no longer consider himself an entelechy of body, soul and spirit but only body and soul because I shall relegate the human spirit to a mere intellectual quality in their small minds."

"What, what are you talking about?" Amelia asked confused.

"Why the destruction of mankind of course. Nation against nation, and kingdom against kingdom." The Devil said proudly.

"But how will we live? What will we do?"

Amelia questioned.

"There is no living without me and you shall do as you're told... sign the book." Satan lashed out in I and thou clarity.

Amelia fell to her knees and the book slammed to the floor.

"The pain." Amelia said. "I have to stop the pain. Let's do it, please."

"Those are the beginning of birth pains Amelia. Sign the book."

"Click."

The pain stopped and Amelia, breathing heavily, lifted herself up. The height dazed her and she stumbled forward catching herself on the arm of the lazy-boy. She picked the serpents tongue up, lifted her slip-dress and froze. The silence was unusual. She started to look up at Lucifer when she felt a strange sensation. A feeling as if being watched. She cared little about what he thought as long as she could satisfy her lust. 'Watch you bastard,' she thought. But it was a different feeling. Etchy in memory as if fading away. Amelia eyes bulged. She threw the flesh to the floor and it rolled under a table. She turned around just as Bob walked from a shadow.

***

The doors opened one hour and seventeen minutes ahead of schedule. As the mist cleared, Bridgette was wheeled out into the airy apartment. She sat in a large monolith block, sculpted to resemble a chair. An electrocardiograph hookup intended for direct use rather than radio transmission, wires were stamped to her chest. Another machines wires attached to Bridgette's head monitored her stereoscopic vision. The movements transmitted images to a motion picture camera for recording and then relayed that image onto the display screens that hung overhead inside the laboratory. The life support alterative was pulled from Bridgette's mouth by one of the medical robots. It had three long stems ejecting from a round base. Its shaved bottom rolled close to the floor. The three limbs had six finger grippers. There were no eyes, no head, just sensors as it rolled back into the lab with plastic tube in grip.

Another robot with two bony arms stuck to the sides of its head took the suction tabs from Bridgette's temples and slid the headgear, which had one strap across the crown of her head and around the chin from her forehead. Its body was shaped like a tin garbage can with six universal wheels at the bottom. It spoke in a digital code which Bridgette frowned at.

"If you can't speak the language," Bridgette announced. "then get the hell out of the country."

Another robot which shape held no imagination was formed to resemble a chalk board. With no arms it wheeled past Bridgette spinning and turning until its black board faced her. It printed up: "ATTENTION: YOU MUST UNDERGO A SYSTEMS ANALYST CHECK BEFORE DEPARTURE. THIS IS STANDARD PROCEDURE. ATTENTION..."

"I don't need a checkup you idiot." Bridgette said as she stood. "I feel fine."

The robot reached for the suction tab on her chest and Bridgette kicked it. The medical robot fell to the floor squealing in digital noises with its wheels rolling around on its bottom.

Bridgette was five-foot ten, with a great
deal of Clairol auburn hair which sprang
energetically as she stood, from a perfect
forehead and coils messily down over her
narrow shoulders. She had a widow's peak.
Lips that would make every man want to taste.
Swan neck. An arch to her back something
most models pose to get.   Young breast
without a care. A Saint-Torpez tan with a
downy sheath that shimmered over her color.

She gently pulled the tab from her chest
and let the wire fall to the floor. Bridgette
took two steps and fell on her face. The three
armed robot made an attempt to help her up
but she fiercely pushed it away. She stood,
taking small petite steps balancing herself on
the arm of the monolith chair. She fell again.

Bridgette raised her buttocks high in the air

and pushed off on her hands to a full stand. The medical robots watched. The sensors in her nose picked up a peculiar smell. The odor here strong enough to stop her abruptly, as if someone had slammed a door in her face. She fanned her nose.

"I smell gas." Bridgette claimed.

The robots turned and ran into one another then disappeared into the lab.

"Mommiamia. Who cut the cheese around here?" Bridgette asked holding her nose.

The chalkboard robot wheeled out and began to print another message but Bridgette stopped it with a wave of her hand. "I know, I know... a system analyst check."

Bridgette sat down in the chair and it rolled back into the lab with the chalk board medical robot close behind. The clock again ticking backwards as the doors closed.

***

"Bob... you're looking good." Amelia cooed.

Bob smiled showing his teeth which made him look young and mischievous and somehow in command again as if his view of the world were the right one, the only civil version around. Amelia drew in her bottom lip and let it roll off her teeth seductively. She began to rub her hips as if inpatient and threw the hair from her face with a jerk of her head.

"Yeah," Bob said as he blew on his fingers and then held them out in front of him. "I've been working out."

Amelia's shoulders slumped and her eyes narrowed as she sneered. "I hate you." She said.

"So I guess the weekend in Paris is off." Bob shot back.

Amelia marched up to Bob with a scolding look on her face. Bob stepped back holding out a stiff arm.

"Wait!" Bob shouted. "I didn't mean to get smart or anything. I have an idea that may..."

Amelia's pace quickened as Bob's plea tripled as if played several times its normal speed.

"satisfy both our interest. How about a trip?" Bob continued.

Amelia was all over him. Pulling his coat off one arm and Bob pulling it back up. She reached inside the coat and squeezed his buttocks roughly while she pressed her body to his.

"Amelia, you really ought' to cut back on your caffeine intake." Bob informed her.

Amelia looked directly into Bob's eyes. The fever of the full moon taking over her body and Bob's warmth driving her into a savage fit. She began to grind up against him, and Bob, confused and slightly aroused, allowed it with a few jerking movements of his own as if trying to escape.

"Let's do it." Amelia said sincerely.

Bob tilted his head awkwardly towards Amelia's mouth. He was pinned to her every move and began to enjoy it but was, for some reason, confused by the outburst of emotions.

"By it, you mean copulate?" Bob asked as

Amelia lifted him above her head and slammed Bob to the floor.

She showed perfect white teeth as she looked down at Bob. Amelia grunted and pulled at the cashmere slip-dress. Her chest heaving with each breath as she lifted the dress to her waist. Bob shook a pointed finger from side to side with a look of concern on his face.

"Is this that post-menstrual thing I've heard so much about?" Bob commented.

Bob's eyes almost popped out of its sockets as Amelia leaped on top of him tearing at the stone-wash jeans zipper. Bob let out a grunt from the air pushed out of his lunges.

A pair of yellow lights glowed high above Amelia's head. The pain came again and Amelia lashed out slapping Bob across the face. She doubled and rolled off him.

Bob lifted himself on one elbow as Amelia lay next to him clutching her stomach in pain.

"This is even too kinky for you Amelia." Bob admitted. "Something's wrong with this picture and I think you need to see a doctor."

"No!" A deep voice emerged shaking the floor. Bob picked himself up looking into the area of the sound.

"Did you see that Amelia. That statue moved." Bob said as he pointed upward.

Amelia clutched at Bob's coat, bringing herself to stand beside him.

"Bob," Amelia said. "I have something to tell you."

The look they both shared some time ago returned as he studied her. Amelia's eye's flushed with every imaginable emotion, gazed sorrowfully into his. Was it her vulnerability or her obvious need he wanted to question?Her seductive appeal or perhaps her intoxicating voice that lulled him senseless. He only knew that he had to keep her talking. To establish some sort of bond with her. To assume anything at this point would be beheading as Bob thought about the slap to his face.

"You exchanged my Hungarian roasted coffee for instant." Bob answered.

For some reason Bob was ready to avoid a roundhouse slap as he blinked from a response so natural to him. But the blow never came. In its stead was the look.

"No Bob, please." She said in a forgiving voice.

Bob watched Amelia closely as both arms were wrapped around her body. Her eyes were crying out to him. Her lips partially spread and her make-up smeared as if she was forced into something against her will. She was asking for help and Bob looked deeper. Deeper inside himself knowing that this was indeed unusual for Amelia and for her, in the state of theory, needed him in a way she couldn't bind herself to ask.

"The pain." Bob asked. "It's not your pain but the pain of something or someone else."

"It is a self-induced inflection." The voice said above them.

"Amelia," Bob noted surprisingly. "that statue is talking to us."

The voice continued. "A theocracy of my own creation, a religion born in blood. I am its creator; its sole purpose is death."

"That's no statue." Amelia said.

Bob frowned. "Who talks like that?"

"Forgive me," The Devil bowed in shrouded darkness to which only Amelia could see clearly. "it is a social blunder to allow the story, much like a giddy child to jump ahead of himself. I am Lucifer. Dishonest, deceitful, treacherous and often unkind."

"Excuse me," Bob said. "but have we met?"

"Through the projection of your unconscious fears." The Devil answered back.

"I still can't place you although the name is familiar. Any relation to the Kansas City Lucifer's?" Bob asked.

"I am the two horned beast whom revelation predicts will incarnate on this planet in flesh and blood to deluge mankind with its technological genius and terrestrial magic, to lead them into the hands of the second appearance of the leviathan, the great dictator of the coming world power."

"I got it." Bob snapped his fingers. "The New Orleans Lucifer's. I'd know that Cajun scent anywhere. It's a cross between gumbo and you using the stove as your personal toilet." Bob laughed.

"I have no time for such trivia." Satan shouted. "I have other important matters that detain me."

The Devil spread his arms and looked down at Amelia. "Sign the book."

Amelia looked nervously around as if lost. It had all became clear. His intention to cut the world from all spiritual development.Her irreversible hand in his retarded aims to destroy and attack by magical forces, brought on the onslaught and materialized world catastrophes and predictions. She had been used and gained nothing and still he insisted on the signing of the book.

"I refuse." Amelia said as she backed away from them both.

Satan pointed a twisted finger at Bob with a nail so torn and aged it looked as if it were a unearth fossil.

"Amelia," Satan pronounced. "I shall do away with thee if thou shalt not covenant with me."

"Hold up, time out, flag on the play, clipping and foul. Where are we going with this fellah? Thou and thee, do away. Sounds too much like wrong Romeo." Bob huffed.

"This has nothing to do with you or what you perceive to be poetic." Satan said evenly. "She must covenant with me or die. It is as simple as your intellectual psychic will allow."

"That's where you're wrong fellah. She's

not going to any convent, she's not even catholic. And even if she were it would kill us both." Bob said calling his bluff.

"So be it." The Devil spat.

"Who talks like that?" Bob asked again.

"Bob," Amelia swallowed. "you don't know what you're saying or who you're dealing with."

Bob looked over his shoulders at Amelia. "Baby, I'm about to throw this bum out. No offense fellah but you're out of here."

Bob casually turned and peered through the darkness.

"None taken." The Devil answered as he reached down and slapped Bob across the room.

Amelia's temper raised in the form of

moderate fits. She was now in a chronic state, on the line to consent in the covenant with the Devil and with solemn assertions to denie him.

She pounded her fist in hand and threw them to her side. Amelia used many explanations and excuses but now he, Satan, had crossed the line.

"Don't anybody slap my man but me." Amelia scowled as she marched up to Satan.

The Devil picked her up by the body and brought her to his lips and kissed her. It was in her nature to strike those that held her, yet an attack aimed outward was of no use as her arms were bound. Amelia spat in his face. At any other time she would laugh immediately, but this one episode using all endeavors to make away with herself and doing mischief unto others, available impulses were squeezed from her body.

Satan laid Amelia down and from his hand poured salt around her body. Salt was unlucky for witches. It held them to that area of real-estate forever unless moved by a mortal or persons not known of that nature.

"Amelia," Bob yelled as he ran through dozens of spotted lights casting nightmare-like shadows around the colossal room. "I didn't break a thing." Bob said childishly. "He slapped me across the room and I weaved, dodged and twisted around all our stuff."

Bob stood over Amelia and the Devil slyly positioned himself for an attack.

"I didn't break a thing." Bob said again.

Bob reached down and with his finger stabbed through the pile of white salt and tasted it. He quickly remembered the distinct flavor and swallowed. His body straightened, his eyes narrowed. Amelia awoke, breathing tiredly as from a long rest and looked up at Bob. They studied each other briefly with Amelia clutching at the chest of her slip-dress.

"If I've told you once Amelia," Bob said. "I've told you a hundred times. Salt substitute. Use a salt substitute. I can't make it any plainer."

"Look at her." The Devil suggested. "If thou have eyes to see, she has deceived me and may thee."

Bob snapped his fingers and pointed up to the Devil. Amelia sat up, straining to see into the shadow from where Satan spoke.

"Barbantio." Bob claimed sharply.

The Devil snorted, tired and inpatient. The heavy smoke wafted through the room from his nostrils as he was again ready to strike.

"You know, Shakespeare's Othello. Barbantio, in a scene from Othello said that to the black Moor. Not in those words I think but pretty close. Then Othello says: My life upon her faith! Honest Iago, my Desdemona must I leave to thee. I prither, let thy wife attend to her, and bring them after in the best advantage. Come," Bob reached out towards Amelia. "Desdemona, I have but an hour of love, of worldly matters and direction, to spend with thee. We must obey the time."

The time was no less apparent to Amelia than Bob in the largest possible terms. The time in which he questioned and easily found a scientific arsenal of strategies and instruments to deal with the situation, to take her to the moon, to consider belonging to the realm of unconscious fantasy, of dreams and reality.

He loved her. As they were both conscious of each other's imperfections, thinking worldly it was perfectly obvious to everyone else or blaming themselves because they were the most convenient targets to blame, closed the door to their differences.

Amelia reached for him. Her fingers tenderly etching toward the border of her prison. The prison she held onto for fear of being touched, held then later rejected. The guards she put in front of her body when in fact she needed none. The door had closed and all that were left were the two.

Electricity struck her fingers and Amelia drew them back. Bob hadn't seemed to notice as his eyes widened in tender repose, luring her to reach out again, and she did. Blue and red flashes leaped out between them as Amelia strained to touch him.

Amelia held back a scream as she closed her eyes tightly. A current circled then struck her forcing her hand back to her side. The Devil laughed at the diabolical element he placed between them. The conspiracy against typical respect.

"I've changed Amelia, I really have." Bob said sincerely. "I even like your friend although I don't understand why he hit me. I didn't even see it coming."

Bob sorted through the shadows imaging what he looked like and feeling awkward knowing he had to make a convincing apology.

"Excuse me." Bob called out. "If I've offended you... I'm sorry. Just step down off that statue and we can square things away over a couple of brewskies. What do you say... friends?"

Bob stuck out his hand. A limber shadow ebbed in the darkness appearing to hover like a projected dream inside his head. It moved swiftly, lumbering towards him striking Bob over his entire body. The blow had tremendous weight behind it sending Bob crashing into a six-foot brass case that housed the 24-karat gold treasures of Tutankhamun.

The decorated regal colors of the young Egyptian Kings priceless treasures were tarnished and faded but prized by Amelia as she gasped. The brass bars caved in as the top row of dramatic sculptures toppled to the floor. Bob pushed the pieces aside sitting a golden Sphinx upright. His mood was deteriorating but he was determined to show Amelia just how serious he really was and made another scrupulous attempt to apologize.

His body ached as he stood. Bob's knees almost gave in as he tried to walk. He had never experienced any type of pain before. He was always ready to react, his reflexes constantly sharp. Even when Amelia struck her blow, it would hurt somewhere deep inside of him. His heart becoming heavy creating a feeling of not wanting to live because of the pain being to much to bare.

'This Viking,' Bob thought oddly, 'put feeling behind this.'

He treasured Amelia and knew of men and their strange appetite for her but he had slain them all; sipped their life from their bodies so they would pursue her no longer. Bob's jealousies grew as he walked twenty-feet back into the area where he was struck. 'For this to be a new start,' Bob thought, 'I would have to place all feeble jealousies aside. She is my princess and she loves me. I have to get this right.'

"Okay," Bob stuck out his hand again. "howbout' a shot of whisky, a man's drink."

The Devil struck out at Bob again but missed. Bob ducked under the shot catching a slight glimpse of the object that sped over him, almost snatching him up in the whirl of its jet stream.

"Ha," Bob measured with index finger and thumb. "missed me by that..."

He saw a figure neither man or beast amorphous in the darkness step from the shadows. His tail end thumping against the floor as it lashed out towards Bob hitting him in the stomach then up to his chin. Bob rolled over several times striking a crippled pose under a 19th century scenery painting by Monet.

Bob continued. "... much."

A voice, gravelly and old with a hint of vibrato shook the ancient statues making ivory and wood African masks rock from their foundations.

"This has been an intoxicating experience," The Devil said. "but in order to pour my embracing wisdom to deluge mankind I will take what I need and go."

Satan stepped into the spotted oval lights which lengthened his horned shadow to Bob's feet. Lucifer offered his hand and spoke somewhat surly of himself. "You will sign the book or be skinned alive."

"Will I be free of you then?" Amelia asked. "Then will I be free of you?"

Bob crouched as if he were to sprint from a runners mark.

"To sign the book," The Devil concluded. "is to covenant with the dead. You shall live forever with me whether you sign the book or not. The ground shall open and send your soul straight to eternal damnation. In hell, you will experience a freedom never offered to you. We've wasted enough time, come with me Amelia."

Bob leaped forward like a cat pouncing on a bird. He rolled over twice, and in standing, drew the double-edge crusader.

It was knocked from his hand flipping ceremoniously like the legendary sword of King Arthur as it was thrown into the waters. The sword pierced an Italian painting by Piero Della Francesca, as Bob was struck again. And again Bob reacted to the challenge repeating over and over again that he would not let anyone take Amelia away from him. It was a powerfully courageous effort to stand in battle with the beast who sought to take over the Earth.

Amelia tried jumping through the circle but the field of captivity pushed her back. She fell to her knees pounding the floor with her fist sobbing for it to end.

Bob wobbled on uneven legs, his forehead taking the full thudding force of a blow. He fought for balance, his head throbbing with pain, his eyes straining to focus as he reached for something, anything to ward him off and finding nothing. Then he fell heavily to the floor and rolled onto his back, moaning from the dull, pounding ache inside his head. Only seconds later he looked up towards the ceiling and saw the bottom of Satan's scalding, blistering foot towering down on him. He caught a curved toe and its flesh cut into his hand like tiny razors. Bob felt the floor beneath him give slightly from the pressure and his ears popped as if descending from an elevator that missed every floor. The veins pushed out at his neck as he buckled his legs, pushing at great strains to save his life.

Satan jested no longer. With shallow effort he pressed Bob into the wood and concrete underneath. As a devious emphasis, the Devil twisted the ball of his foot into the hole creating a deeper imprint, an imprint into Amelia's mind and spirit as she covered inside her arms.

"Stop Lucifer, please stop." Amelia cried out. "I will sign your stupid book if this will please you. Just let him go. He's done nothing to you."

"There is a suspicious amount of pity in your voice for this creature. It is unlike you

Amelia. But since your laconic response pacifies my vision, the battle between darkness and light will never-the-less proceed with or without you. The more blood I spill the more retarded mans spiritual forces become. This one is of no use to you or I. It is dead by the sole of my inflection. He is no more."

Satan lifted his foot, turned and walked towards Amelia. Bob lay pressed, mingled with splinters, blood and matrix, but was far from dead. The rivalry far from over. He would not rest or let Amelia go after countless attempts to stop Lucifer.

Bob straightened his legs and the bones snapped back into their sockets. Satan turned around, his eyes blazing sunset orange as Bob popped his neck into place. Bob stood, his body battered, his clothing, which he always kept fastidious, looked like they had been slept in for a week, brushed clean what he could and met Satan's stare.

"Had enough?" Bob asked defiantly.

Satan's tail whipped across the floor, tripping furniture and columns, breaking glass and thin oak legs. Bob leaped high into the air, flipping twice avoiding the sharp pointed end of Satan's tail. Bob landed on his feet and ran towards the sword. Satan's tail lashed out again over Bob's head but he slid on both knees across the floor stopping under the double-edge crusader that was now hanging above him. One side of Bob's body strained as he pulled the sword from the wall. He jumped to his feet, thrashing the crusader in an all-round weapon sword-play stance. The Devil eyed the blade just as Amelia once had.

In the apartment lights which shone on the edges of the sword, Satan heard faint echoes of the battle between darkness and light. He could feel the blatant screams of dark intelligence and see it being poured into caldrons boiling over onto flesh-less skulls. Bob waved it in front of his face and Satan's eyes followed.

"You make your death rewarding." Satan said as he stood erect. "The imperial sword was thought thrown into a volcano yet it gleams as if just folded. It would be an honor to peel the flesh from your body with such a collection in hand."

"Who wants to live forever." Bob replied.

The serpents tongue inched across the floor in front of Bob. He eyed it curiously and raised a foot slamming it with all the pressure he could into the tarnished wood missing the serpents tongue by inches. It moved to its left. Bob tried again and again it jerked out of his foots hammering reach. Again Bob tried and several times it jetted left, right, then it moved in circles as if teasing him, letting Bob know it knew his every thought. Bob twirled the blade around his hand and sliced it through the air. It split the serpents tongue in two pieces. Satan howled like a large wild animal caught in a trap. The mosaic French windows smashed into numerous pieces. The fourteen-foot marble statue of David cracked in three particle blocks, rolling on the floor like a great boulder from an avalanche. Other statues began to break; bronze, gold and the wood covered Guan Yin split causing the gem to fall from its forehead.

Yellowish-green waste spilled from Satan's mouth burning speckled-like holes in the wood flooring as Bob was thrown off his feet. Paintings fell and glass cases shattered.

Satan stormed out of the room, running in mystical gallops under the lights, knocking over whatever was in his path. Bob picked himself up and walked over to the stains that were frying like acid on skin. With his sword, he lifted a Persian rug and flipped it over. To his right he picked up the corner to another and tossed its edge aside.

Bob walked over the wood floor and it squeaked and whined from his weight. Parts of the floor cracked underneath him and he steadied himself. The wood rotted away from apparent neglect. The stains were everywhere.

Amelia touched a hand to her chest. Bob's mesmerizing bedroom eyes changed dramatically as their gazes met, becoming what she could only term as homicidal.

A large brick wall seemed to fall on him in their silent stare. The pieces began to fit as he wished the floor would open up and swallow him whole. He actually looked down at his feet, hoping.

Bob turned his back to Amelia squinting his eyes. The past rushing through his mind like total recall to a computer. The feverish nights he caught her accompanying the flesh inside her. Trust me as she walked out into the night with no explanation. An explanation-he deserved at least that much, but now it was too late for excuses. As naive as he had been it was all too obvious now. She preferred sexual intercourse with a two-ton evil. The evil stabbed him in the back and it was not him-the himthat name faded from his memory, but her... Amelia. The distrust, the lies; 'the bitch.' He thought. If he couldn't have her then no one would.

He turned around facing Amelia again for

what he urged himself would be the last time. Her full name sat on the tip of his tongue, the frontal lobes of his memory until it was the only thing echoing through his brain. She looked at Bob as if she knew. Amelia feared he'd kill her, him, or both.

There was no begging in her eyes which he thought made it easier as he lifted his head as if that would allow his mouth to fall open. 'It would either kill her or possess her,' he could hear the doctor say over and over again inside his head, deleting the pounding in his ears like the harsh hammering of a judges gavel to which he thought was an oncoming headache but was in fact Satan's return.

Bob did not see or sense Lucifer as he stood beside Amelia. Only the harsh laughter followed by throat, grabbing words and Amelia, who broke the hypnotic stare, had

Bob realized where he was.

"I am the beast," The Devil proclaimed. "and was given a mouth to utter proud words and blasphemies and to exercise his authority and I shall. I am followed by the unseen coming with dark principalities and powers which will inspire a demonic reign of terror and cold-blooded butchery outstripping in primitive savagery and bestial cruelty. All previous ages of tyranny and oppression in the entire history of mankind follow me this day: the white horse, the red horse, the black horse, and the pale horse of death. I am and will be the death of you."

Satan slammed a solitary iron spearhead, black with age into the tarnished wood floor. Its long tapering point was supported by a wide base with metal flanges depicting the wings of a dove. Within in a central aperture of the blade a hammer-head nail secured by a cuff threaded with gold, silver, and copper wire. On the side of the lowest portion of the base, golden crosses were embossed.

In the dark reaches of his mind he could hear the doctor say: "He will have this."

***

Bridgette underwent everything from biological control to track and field. She ran in place on the treadmill saying over and over to herself, "I am not a lab mouse, I am not a lab mouse."

Her silk dressing gown which was only tied at the neck separated by the jaunting movements of her arms exposing her breast. They were larger than she imagined and watched the hefty muscles bounce fully in the reflection of the observation windows. She wanted him to see what he had perfected. She wanted him to burn with desire his body pressed so hard against the one-way glass that it would leave a impression affixed to the pane. She tried to create a memory but couldn't. She didn't know how. The track slowed then stopped. She moved her head from side to side which automatically stored her features to memory. A normal function she didn't realize happened.

She parted the gown eyeing the patch of black pubic hair hoping he would catch a glimpse, closed it teasingly.

Bridgette allowed, this time, the two armed bucket, she called it, to check her pulse and remove the suction tabs. An example of the biotelemetry radioed to the record display showed even lines interrupted by a short line upward and a longer one downward as if someone were trying to draw a straight line in the back seat of a small speeding car. The two armed robot tore the readout from the electrocardiograph and wheeled away.

Bridgette stepped from the treadmill and turned her back to the windows. The medical robot wheeled by her and she stopped it by gripping the top of its shinny, grayish, bald head and easily picked it up. She could hear the wheels spinning. Out of curiosity she applied the seven-hundred pounds of foot pressure given to her and squeezed which looked as gentle as holding a balloon tightly until the crunching chimes of thin metal was heard. Her thumb punched through the globe and automatically a thought entered her mind commanding a better view enhanced the area around her thumb until she could see the meaningless gears and mechanisms from the small hole by the thumb nail. She dropped the robot to the floor holding it steadily in one place. The wheels grinding against the wood. The friction causing smoke to twirl from underneath it.

The robot squealed in mechanical codes. Bridgette's eyesight returned just as quickly as it had magnified. She wanted more details, more input on how she worked and what else she could do. But more importantly, her sex. The thought made her smile lightly. She wanted to turn around, to see if he was watching. But this was not what she wanted him to see.

Bridgette parted the gown and stuck out a slender leg which bared her body from the waist down. Unknowingly, in digital code. "Does this thing work?" She asked demurely, almost sweetly in digital language as she pointed to the half inch strands of pubic hair.

The robot answered in digital codes. "INFORMATION DISK.INFORMATION DISK."

"Yes." She said awkwardly at a blank space in front of her.

Bridgette released the medical toy. It ran squealing into the wall, bounced off and tipped over. The information disks that sat behind Professor Marcus. That would tell her all she needed to know. Another smile wet her lips as she walked towards the sliding doors. They opened as Bridgette looked as if she would walk through them if they didn't, stepped out into the airy apartment, and unlike a robot, looked around casually. The recliners back was aimed at Bridgette. She could see his arms laid out over the arms rest as if he were asleep. Exhausted after a long day.

A sensation bubbled up inside her close to her heart. She placed a hand there and in feeling the steady ba-bump, ba-bump quicken, smiled brightly. Her porcelain teeth set a sparkling glimmer in her eyes as they slanted happily. He had worked a miracle, she thought. Her first emotional feeling... I think. She wasn't sure but it wasn't there before.

She inhaled. Her breast heaving proudly outward pushing against the silk gown. She held it gently as if pledging to the allegiance and with her small hands squeezed. Nothing.

She felt the pressure of her hand but thought there would be something more. She remembered the movies. The one-thousand disk were the answer. Professor Marcus would be slow, shy and timely in a response. A gentleman, she amused herself in thought.

Nice and slow. She liked that.

"Is that you Marcus, or am I experiencing artificial reality?" She asked gently.

Bridgette walked up to the chair and turned it around. She saw what she saw. And what she recorded in less than a nano-second made no sense. Her head jerked to the left. Her mind recorded a chemical analysis of the stain on Doctor Marcus shirt. Her head jerked upward, right, then straight ahead. Window pane missing, computer inoperative, epee tip analyzed; clean. Wound, not self inflicted, 998 disk two missing. Foot prints, two sets. First set confirmed... Doctor Marcus DeShay. Second set... 175 lbs., 6'1.753", rubber soles size 10.5 D worn heel on right foot. Plasmatic residue matrix: table, light, chair, knee, shoulder, window, and windows edge. Bridgette's eyes highlighted every area called out. DNA analysis... diversified constituents. Unable to determine biological structure from this data.Classification... non-human.

Bridgette calmly and without emotion turned to the racks of disks. She peeled and folded a layer of skin on the left side of her neck, pulled out the first disk and inserted it into the slot. Her ocular bulbs blinked, changing color from smeary pink to flashing red. The disk was being recorded.

***

"I am Lucifer. The shatter of worlds."

Satan began to speak in tongues passing the talisman of power from one hand to the other. Bob looked on. Not really hearing him but appearing to give it his undivided attention, simply and irretrievably focused on Amelia, and drifted. His thoughts were incoherent and in his daze of dream verses reality with the dream yet taking form, the reality struck Bob in the chest.

He stammered backwards trying to distinguish between the two evils of what was really happening and what could possibly be an illusion. He felt heavy, faint. Sweat beaded on his upper lip as he fought to speak. The wooden end of the spear reached out several feet in front of him. Bob dropped the sword clutching the talisman as he pulled effortlessly at its removal.

Amelia jumped up pressing hard against the invisible wall that imprisoned her. Her hands pushed through as electrified waves jetted up her arms completing a wrinkled texture over her skin turning Amelia into a life escaping corpse. She weakened and was thrown back into the circle. She could hear her heart pounding in her ears and see the veins pushing against her pale flesh, the skin gluing together as color and texture returned. With her bodies nerves not yet adjusted, Amelia tried to stand. She crumbled to one knee but steadied herself with both hands on the floor. Amelia's body shook in spurts as if a chill had taken her. She closed her eyes, stood, clasped her hands and concentrated on a spell.

The fire had died considerably, except for the dappled, lethargic shadows created by the dying embers. The light catching Bob's eyes in a hit and miss pattern that made them look like little sputtering fires. Suddenly Satan walked up to Bob and pushed the spear deeper into his chest and out of him came only a ululating, reflexive sound, "Aaaagh."

Amelia's eyes sprang open as Bob fell backwards his body falling slowly to the floor. The spears tip pierced the wood as Bob's body slid down the wooden handle. His arms flung out and his head drooped lifelessly aside.

"Amelia." Bob sobbed softly.

The voice had a multi-directional quality, as if she were thinking rather than hearing.

The Devil looked down at Amelia. "Amelia," he said and offered his hand. "mankind is standing on the brink of the most evil epoch in the entire history of the planet. Let's make a new world, you and I."

Amelia folded her arms and as if wiping the sleep from your eyes, disappeared. Her clothes fell to the floor as if she had just stepped out of them. She appeared again coming up through the flooring outside the circle like some mystical projection. She fluttered past Satan leaving traces of herself behind her as she walked. Her clad body translucent as Satan reached out repeatedly grasping thin air. She knelt over Bob and lifted his head. Amelia bent, her eyes leveling with his. So close were their lips as Amelia breathed a mist into Bob's opened mouth. His eyes opened staring directly into hers. A tear ran down her cheek, a souvenir of what it was like to feel-to feel loss. As she drew closer he noticed that her breath was warm and sweet smelling.

"You are a witch." Bob said weakly.

Amelia nodded yes and the tears fell unto his lips and off his cheek. Bob's eyes closed as his head slacked then went limp. Amelia laid his head down and watched as Bob began to die, leaving only a skeleton, the skull which separated at each portal. His jawbone clicking onto the floor in a grotesque rictus while the bones of his fingers turned to dust. The spear fell to the floor and Bob was gone.

Amelia's lifeless apparition floated off the floor leaving traces of herself and one by one, in puffs of crystal particles, they vanished.

Amelia floated above Satan's head like some perpetual motion thing with limbs. Her chin was pressed to her chest and arms hung loosely at her sides. A corona backed her as Amelia's body swayed. She mourned as all feeling left her body in a stream of salted, unstoppable tears.

"Hey you."

Amelia's body jerked as if pushed from the back and she thought she was and turned around. Bob looked up at her smiling brightly.

"Missed me?" He asked in a crystalline

tenor.

"I miss you so much I could kill you." She said. "And I meant that in the nicest way."

"I'd hate to know how you felt if you hated me and I hope I never do." Bob said whole-heartily.

"Enough." Satan yelled. "This is treason. Amelia, come."

Amelia smiled and opened her arms tilting her head romantically left.

"Father." She said, her eyes slapping towards criminal.

Bob took off his coat and threw it on the floor. The stain still visible as he ripped the sweat-shirt from his body. It too fell to the floor in torn pieces. He began to breath heavily, his nostrils flared as his body began to change. His hair fell out and small horns pierced through the top of his skull. His eyes sunk deep into their sockets and his brow thickened. Bob's spine pushed out of his skin and large wings with sharp claws at the tips split the sides of his back advertising what he was about to become. He angled his head and growled inwardly as a dollop of drool etched from the corner of his mouth. His wings began to flap wildly as his body lengthened and muscles tightened and rippled. Another pair of arms dropped from underneath his arm pits, the knuckles barely touching the floor. His feet were long and nails curved on his feet as well as his fingers. The shoes shreds of unrecognizable leather were still tied awkwardly to a small portion around his fallen arches and the top of his purplish-gray foot.

Bob hissed exposing small fangs, sharp and pearl white over chapped blue lips. He pushed out his chest, leaned his head back until gristle snapping sounds as if chewing on bones erupted from his mouth.

Satan watched. No more amused than the thousand times he instituted death. The Devil looked as if expecting it, not surprised at all.

Amelia, with arms stretched wide, floated towards Satan's face. The Devil thought she would only go through him, and she appeared to or so it seemed. She hugged his face covering his eyes but Satan could see through her. She melted into him and stood naked inside Satan's mind. She swiftly drew her pawl and chain as she knew this was no place to be for long and slung it into the dark curves of his mind. Quickly Satan let out a scream and blasphemous insults. The pawls edges showed through his skull as the pawl slowly cut at him.

Bob picked up the crusader and stabbed Satan in the stomach. Satan's tail lashed out and Bob flew over it. The tail commanding Bob's attention as it whipped at an attempt to keep him away. Bob guarded against it trying to slice the fifteen-foot reptile's ass from catching him with its sharp, pointed tip.

Amelia stood inside Satan's head with her hands on her hips, pleased. She heard squeaking sounds and wondered if in between the noise she could hear Satan's pleas for mercy. But she shook the thought away and in knowing Lucifer fully he would undergo far more than this and would never surrender. She began to put another plan to her thinking when in the flickering lights of the pawl grinding against the chain she saw a flow of something dark and wavy coming towards her. Amelia reached down and picked up loose parts of the chain in case she needed to recall the spinning pawl. Her eyes strained to see and she thought maybe she was straining to much. What she saw coming towards her made her stiffen. Flowing and running over themselves in an attempt to get at her were rats. Hundreds upon thousands of large hairy beasts.Their tiny blood-shot eyes darting, blinking like the hold button on a telephone. Amelia dropped the chain and left. She appeared screaming at the top of her lungs.

"Rats! Rats!!" She yelled and dove through the floor.

Satan pulled his hands from over his ears.

"Rats." Bob said. "Is that from the movie Willard?"

Satan slapped Bob across his body sending him flying across the room. Bob's wings flapped, slowing his body until he floated by his own power. Satan reached for the talisman but Bob quickly brushed it away with a sweep of his wings. Lucifer straightened his body and drew back an arm. Satan released his blow but Bob charged him slicing Satan's arm off at the shoulder. Satan, in mock surprise stared at his arm which jerked as if it had been stung by electricity.

Amelia came through the floor slowly occupying her slip-dress as her body stemmed upward through the circle. She saw Satan's hand flexing on the floor. A green spill burning into the wood from the cut portion of the arm. Bob took that spell binding opportunity and cut off Satan's head. Bob chopped off the other arm then sliced the legs away near the hips. His torso slammed to the floor with his head rolling over and over making a bobbling sound as if a child's toy were rolling on square wheels.

"Ouch, bet that hurt." Bob teased as he landed gently on his feet.

He looked over to Amelia. She was still caught up in the moment of Satan's riddled remains when her eyes bulged. She was still inside the circle when she pointed to the floor. Bob frowned. His throat dry as he opened and closed his mouth to induce the saliva that would moisten it.

From the six parts of Satan's body emerged small four foot creatures. They were in likeness of the Devil but childish. Their eyes lacked the sparkle of youth, as if their tear ducts were missing. Each small creature had peeled back their colorless lips revealing razor-pointed canines. Bob swallowed and raised the crusader over his head. They leaped on top of him before he could go through with his attempt. They sunk their teeth into his legs, his stomach, his now quivering carotid.

Bob ran through the apartment, back and

forth in front of Amelia yelling. "Get these little blood suckers offa' me."

Bob stopped in front of Amelia and fell to his knees. His wings flapped furiously and all four arms pulled to get them off. The wind from his wings blew the salt from Amelia. She stepped closer and snapped her fingers. Bob turned to stone and the demons fell to the floor and scurried off into the shadows laughing and whispering childishly. Amelia stepped back and with both hands framed Bob as she squinted through one open eye.

Bob was frozen with eyes wild and hands reaching for his throat while his wings receded back and his other arms stretched outward.

"I like it." She agreed comically.

Amelia could hear faint rumbling sounds coming from the statue of Bob. She walked up to it and bent over him bringing an ear close to Bob's head. She knocked twice and the statue cracked open. Bob stood and dusted the plaster off of him. His wings folded neatly behind him. The clawed tips angling over his head.

"Very funny Amelia." Bob said with a smirk.

Amelia put a fist to her lips and giggled.

"You still love me?" She asked.

"Love doesn't go just like that." Bob snapped with his fingers.

"You forgive me... right?" Amelia questioned bright-eyed.

"Hell no!" Bob said and walked away from her.

Bob returned holding two Remington pistol-grip sawed-off pump shotguns and two nylon shotgun shell belts with quick release buckles strapped across his body over his shoulders. He looked out into the apartment with a hint of danger in his eyes. His oblong head bent slightly as he put on a pair of Rayban sunglasses.

"Let's rock."

Agessander, Athenodorus, and Polydorus of Rhodes. The eight-foot marble statue of the Laocoon Group was just ahead of Bob but there was an extra head seated alongsidePolydorus. Bob pumped a shell into the shotguns chamber, aimed and fired shattering the shoulder and head of Athenodorus. He fired again missing the small Devil completely but catching Polydorus' left side. Chips of the statue fell to the floor as Bob pumped cartridges into the chambers again.

One shotgun was aimed to his left and one

to his right as Bob walked and fired at anything that moved. Bob stood in the center of the room spreading foam material and wood into the air as the pit sofa accepted three shotgun blast. The barrels smoked as he loaded them quickly. One creature sat upon the 2nd century bronze statue of Wu Wei's Flying Horse and another clamped its claws into the eight-by-fourteen oak paneling above a selected painting by Van Gogh.

"Wise choice." Bob said as he let loose a flurry of shotgun blast, eight in all shredding Goya, Greco, Van Gogh and Rembrandt. The Han Dynasty's Flying Horse was only recognizable by a hoof attached to its base. Shiva Nataraja would never be restored as it was crippled beyond repair.

The demons laughed, running, crawling and jumping about trying to seek refuge but

Bob had leveled almost everything. His lazy-boy rocked and he shot that too. He began to reload as Amelia, standing unmoved outside the blown away circle, walked up to Bob and removed the glasses. She smiled lightly and walked behind him.

They gathered one-hundred feet in front of Bob sure of themselves holding the ancient weapon associated with the legend of the worlds destiny. It had witnessed many scenes in its passage through two-thousand years of history, but perhaps never so strange a setting as this.

Bob smiled nonchalantly and leveled each shotgun. One high and the other low. The demon holding the talisman threw it up and caught it as if preparing to distance throw the javelin. Bob split the shotguns and shot at the two that held the four in the middle catching them full in the chest sending them hurdling against the wall with a thud. He pumped and tried again decapitating the demon who arched the talisman behind it. Before the demon dropped to the floor and the others could run he slaughtered them all, the shots echoing out as their bodies decor the walls and the floor. Cerise stains were everywhere and the talisman lay in a shimmering pool of the purplish-red mixture.

Bob dropped the shotguns, turned to Amelia and hugged her. Amelia pushed him away and spun Bob back around. The bodies began to merge. It turned into a wiggling stem of blood. Skulls pushed out and a dozen arms stretched as if awakening. Objects turned within themselves growing taller, lengthening outward until a familiar shape towered heavily inside the room.

Its voice a little sharper and a lot more baritone than usual laughed heartily.

"Missed me?" Satan asked and threw back his head and laughed again.

"Ah Shit." Was all that Bob could say.

***

She slipped on a pair of black thigh-high nylons and a white bustier skirt with side fringe. She put on a red leather jean jacket and black suede ankle boots with two inch heels. Atop an antique cherry wood dresser were several fragrances. She looked into the mirror and smiled demurely. She combed through her auburn hair letting the silk strands fall over her shoulders. She sprayed three scents over her body stepping back spraying the third into the air and walked into it. She thought her nose was too large and her mouth too narrow. All her skirts were very short but her energy level high as she paraded around the room becoming accustomed to the shoes making the lower part of her skirt snap as her panty-less hips moved this way and that. Her undergarments were thrown around the small room in disarray as she disapproved of the color, style and texture.

Polyester, she frowned, and decided to wear nothing. 'Would he approve?' The thought was wear and the approval left up to her.

She was ready she thought, but not yet. There was something else she had to do. Something of a nature she did not want to face. But it was his request-an almost dyeing wish that was left to her to perform. She waited on the emotional content of her programming but felt nothing. No tears, no bubbling or upsurge of depression as she stalled hoping that she would fall to her knees and cry. Still nothing.

She turned with a sigh and walked from the closet-like room that possessed what was given to her. Bridgette stepped quickly over to the doctor and laid his hands into his lap. The tower blinked, and as if she knew pushed the lever that dislodged the disk inside. Again she peeled back the skin on her neck and inserted the disk.

Bridgette removed the metal grating, picked the doctor up and placed him over the logs. She replaced the gratings, pulled a long match stick from a black and orange cylinder, struck it and set the corner of a log afire. It caught immediately. Bridgette turned a handle which opened the draft doors. She stepped back and watched. The recording finished, Bridgette pulled it from her neck, replaced the skin and threw the disk into the fire.

A puzzle of odors greeted her. She began to analyze each smell: hair, fabric, flesh. Flesh stuck out in her mind as she pushed for a response. Laughter, profanity, anything but nothing came to thought. 'Was I programmed to be this cold?' She questioned. Her instructions were to deal with the elements that caused Abby's death, to burn his body if he died as she did or died period. The smell became hotly sour as Bridgette focused on a blank space on the wall above the fireplace. Her optical processor produced a picture in her mind. The information given to her about Abby. Bridgette watched a coroner roll back one of the deceased's eyelids and train a light onto Abby's eye.

Marcus watched the pupil contract. The coroner let the lid drop and looked down at the body. The deceased fingernails were still pinkish and she looked as if she were sleeping. Linda reaffirmed with other medical staff over and over again that the body on the gurney was, in fact, dead. Except for the pupil contraction she was but it was her job to find the cause. She pushed aside a wayward hair and pulled her lab coat over her exposed left knee. Her hair tied in a bun, horned rimmed glasses and white over-coat gave her an appearance of a middle aged woman. Linda Wilder, took off her glasses and put them in the top pocket of her medical jacket. That gesture took ten years off her as she placed a reassuring hand on Marcus's shoulder. A slight compassionate smile touched the corners of her mouth.

"What do you think?" Linda asked.

Marcus didn't answer. He was mesmerized, caught up in thought, and disbelief. He stared as if looking through Abby and seeing what she felt-at death. His eyes swelling with each sniffle to hold the flood of tears back that he knew soon would be inevitable. There was no one else in the room as she squeezed his shoulder, possibly bringing him back as he jumped slightly. A normal reaction she thought as he was in his own world.

"It's strange, but not unusual." She said.

"Yes, I know." Marcus said calmly.

"So, you've seen this before?"

"No but I've heard about it."

"Oh." Linda said surprised. "Well, I'm about to check the time of death."

"You mean through the, uh, rectum?"

Marcus swallowed.

"Yes."

Marcus looked uncomfortable wetting his lips and adjusting the choke of his shirt. She was pretty sure of herself. Not at all what he expected. A short man with a bad back and hair loss, about sixty-eight years old. No, eighty-six with thick glasses that he had to wipe constantly because of heavy perspiration. She was nothing like that. Always so calm and academic, by the book academic.

"When the heart stops," She said. "the blood will gather at the lowest point, like any liquid would. But I don't have to tell you that Doctor Marcus."

Marcus didn't answer. He just shook his head no.

"Well, when they found her she was as she

is now so it will be easy to check the time of death." Linda said.

She reached over and began to turn over the body. Marcus stopped her.

"The marks on her neck," Marcus said. "what do you think of them?"

Linda put on her glasses and turned the head carefully.

"Snake bite." Linda said. "What do you think they are?"

Snake bite was a good guess and he could sense in her voice that she was doing just that, guessing. The condition of the body, the color, and the pupil contraction were not consistent with her diagnosis. If he gave his opinion, which he wanted to share with someone, he would surely be labeled insane.

"I have no idea." Marcus said. "Your

guess is as good as mine."

"That's not a guess." Linda said in a matter of fact tone. "If that's not what it is, I will find out."

Marcus turned away as Abby was turned over to be checked for lividity. He cleared his throat and pulled a folded paper from the inside breast pocket of his sport jacket. Marcus held the paper out behind him waiting for her to grab it. He peeked over his shoulder as Linda was going over Abby's body. It was, he thought, almost sacrilege.

"This is a court order," Which he forged. "demanding that the body be cremated immediately."

Linda snatched off her glasses and looked curiously at Marcus.

"That's not proper procedure. I have to-"

"It's a court order," Marcus said firmly. "just do it, ASAP."

He slapped the paper into her hand as he turned and walked out of the room pushing the swinging doors making them fan back and forth.

The thought fog cleared. Bridgette turned and walked down the long hallway leading to the elevator. She stood inside; the doors began to meet as she played the track over again. 'Dead, just dead.'

***

"I need a drink."

"What's wrong?" Amelia asked Bob.

"I don't think I can fight him off any

longer. I need blood." Bob said weakly.

Bob's features began to pale and he hunched as if tired. Satan picked up the spear of destiny and held it in both hands. Amelia stood at Bob's side, placed a hand on Bob's chest and inhaled deeply.

"Here" She angled her head, offering her slender throat. "Drink your fill sweetheart." And closed her eyes.

The invitation was too strong to deny. Bob's jaws opened wide. Saliva dripped from the corners of his mouth as he leaned over and tickled her carotid with his fangs. He gasped looking straight into the oval face of the grandfather clock and backed away from Amelia.

"Bob." She implored. "What is it?"

"It's almost time." Bob turned and looked

to the East through the opening in the wall which was once graced by mosaic paine. Satan slowly walked towards them.

"Pick up the sword Bob and throw it at him." Amelia urged.

"I can't. I'm too weak and the sun will be up soon."

"Pick up the sword Bob. Throw it, throw it now."

Bob started to speak. A cloud appeared over the horizon. Amelia picked up the sword and looked at the clock. She turned back to Bob.

"Do it now before it's too late." Amelia begged.

In desperation Amelia did not realize she held the silver blade touching her hand glistening from the overhead lights and the urgencies to destroy Satan. An object used to kill witches: silver and the fire that burned from within when barely touched buy it. She turned Bob around.

"Do it!"

Bob's face was ghost white and his eyes weak with fear and age looked like a lost child. Satan galloped towards them. His hoofed feet thumping on floor and carpet giving his approach a distantly loft sound.

Amelia sliced a deep cut into her open palm. She held the sword back and threw it into Satan's shoulder. Lucifer stammered back pulling at the blade which made a deep impression. Amelia shoved her hand into Bob's mouth. He held on to it, drinking and draining Amelia for the precious mineral.

Satan managed to pull the sword from his arm and threw it behind him. Blood, deep purple, poured from the open wound. Amelia looked down at the stains. They began to turn red. Satan licked the gash closed and leveled the spear aiming it at Bob. Amelia looked into Satan's eyes. They knew what was to happen next.

"Today," Satan voiced. "a third of the world will parish and you, the simple suckling of a parasite will taunt me no longer."

Satan threw the spear of destiny. The blade spun creating a dizzying mirage as it was almost impossible to see. Bob caught the spear releasing Amelia's hand in the same effort. The quick release catches of the shell belt snapped apart as Bob's wings spread twelve feet wide circling them both like an opened umbrella.

"That's Bob." He said proudly.

"Do it now Bob before they come."

Amelia pleaded.

Bob looked down at Amelia, puzzled.

"Why? Did we order out or something?" Bob asked sincerely.

"He's flesh now. Kill him before they come." Amelia sobbed.

Four mystical apparitions seeped through the walls taking on shapes as the ghost white clouds floated around the room. A white horse galloped behind Satan with a white knight sitting on its bare back. Satan lifted a crown and placed it on top of the white knights head, the horse raised on its hind legs kicking its forelimbs. Through the eyes of the headgear were pitch black emptiness. The knight pulled a single arrow from its back and placed it in the bows handle. A red horse and knight appeared. The horse's eyes were brunt red with fire shooting from its nostrils. The red knight held a two handed sword.

From the mist a black knight with a pair of balances held on tightly as the black horse bucked shaking its large head and blowing smoke from its frowned lips. A white fog, stationed in front of Bob and Amelia appeared suddenly. Sitting on the pale horse was a skeleton. Amelia fell to her knees pressing both hands to her ears.

"They're laughing at me." She screamed.

Bob heard it too and looked out into the wide open night. The cloud had thickened and seemed to be moving swiftly in zig-zagging formations. At some points it would open then close and at others it would circle outward then move back in a gathering. Northeastern storms tracked West to East, rarely the opposite as the high pitched laughter, almost like a siren, picked up several octaves as it covered the sky. The pale horse moved beside Satan.

"This time," Satan said. "I have actually incarnated amongst my pupils in a physical body of flesh and blood. I am the progeny of reincarnating generations."

His voice was loud and audible but barely drowning out the high shrill-like laughter that now had Bob clutching his ears.

"The two horned beast of the apocalypse, and your death is here." Satan yelled.

The white knight pulled back the arrow against the taunt bow-string. The red knight approached them slowly arching the two-handed sword above its head. Its armor was as dull as boiling blood. The black knight held up the balances, one out leveled the other. The skeleton which sat upon the pale horse, its macabre grin sent a formidable chill through Bob as he backed away.

A bird flew through the window frightening the red horse. The red knight was thrown off its back and fell soundlessly to the floor. The horse bucked and ran through the wall.

Several birds came through the window flying over the heads of Satan and his followers. The white knight aimed and released the arrow slicing one of the birds wings. It fell to the carpet without a sound. Another arrow appeared in the bows handle and it aimed again just as the room became full of brownish whippoorwills, sparrows with grayish plumage and loons with mottled plumage carrying with them an eerie, laugh-like cry.

The knights and their horses disappeared. Bob covered Amelia with his large wings as thousands of birds entered the room. The cries were unbearable as Satan's flesh was torn away. His laughter was like standing near a tremendous earthquake, a deep rumbling. As each bird pulled some part of Satan from him it left taking that portion of its being to another part of the world.

The towering fifteen-foot beast flesh, muscle, and cartilage was stripped from his body, its bones falling to the floor and carpet as it was lifted by the claws and beaks of thousands of birds and taken out into the night. A bright flash followed.

***

An intern temporarily kept his heart going.

"One, two, three." His hands one pressed

over the other slid the large rimmed glasses back against the bridge of his nose while he waited to complete the repetition.

A nurse with electric defibrillation paddles stood by as a doctor pulled back an eye lid shinning a pen light through the marble-like eye.

"Stand back." She said, handing the paddles to the cardiologist as he quickly moved to the patient's side.

An instrument stand was pushed aside and the bright overhead light was readjusted. The curtains were quickly drawn with each nurse and attendant taking in a deep breath.

"We have something." A nurse in a white lab coat announced professionally.

She had a pair of scissor-like clamps with its circular ends leaning out of the coats top left pocket. Her brunette hair messily over her forehead and shoulders were a result of the emergency departments overcrowding as all eyes searched the electronic equipment that kept records of the patient's blood pressure, heart rate, respiration, and temperature. They settled for the electrocardiograph and waited for the signal.

Nurses report important changes in a patient's condition to a doctor and then carry out the doctor's orders for correcting the situation. Medical school prepared her for every conceivable situation, even this, as at times, dummies and cadavers were substituted with live volunteers. But there were no clear orders for correcting this situation as Bob had his hand nestled between the nurse's thighs.

"No, over here." She managed to say through parted lips. "I believe we have something here." And she pointed between Bob's legs.

Some saw Bob's arm moving in and out as the registered nurse twitched erotically. Others ran their eyes back and fourth watching the behavior that made him stiff.

Bob pushed the panic button and woke up from the dream. He patted his body. He was back to his normal self. Amelia stood over him with a glassy expression. Her eyes darting from his face to somewhere below his waist as he lowered his chin to his chest. He swiftly covered himself out of embarrassment and managed to stand. Amelia's eyes were bright and child-like. She ringed her hands together and breathed evenly.

"I'm not cleaning this shit up." She said smartly.

Bob just smiled. The condominium was up-settled by the mayhem of just one day.

Almost everything they possessed was broken, mangled or shattered in such a manner that it was unrecognizable. Whatever was left was blotted with bird waste. Bob ignored it.

"Come here you." Bob said.

"And how far is that?" Amelia replied looking down at Bob's stiffness, it pressing outward making a mountain-like impression through his torn jeans. A ripped pocket exposed Mickey Mouse's large eyes, its hand at a wave and its face warmly smiling. He grabbed her, pressing his already turgid phallus against her groin.

A knock came at the door. They dismissed it and reached for a kiss. The knock came again but was damagingly brutal as the door fell off its hinges and onto the carpet. Bob and Amelia jumped erratically, startled by the hollowed sounds of each coffin falling like dominos to the floor. The Jacuzzi was drastically shoved aside. The shower walls caved in and the stage mirror with its perimeter lights shattered as it fell sideways tumbling over the bidet. Water shot out through the openings of the ripped out pipes. It was an added conclusion to the day as Bridgette marched with alacrity into the adjoining room stepping over marble blocks, broken chairs, glass and fallen pictures. Her eyes were deadly focused ahead.

"You called a maid?" Bob whispered to Amelia through clinched teeth like a ventriloquist. "How sweet."

"You can start by sweeping that glass up and getting a clean rag and wiping whatever's not spotted with filth. I'll turn off the water so you can mop. Everything you need is in a closet in the back of the apartment. I'll show you." Bob clarified, stepping away from Amelia.

Bridgette stepped up to Bob and placed her fists on her hips.

"And who was your slave last week?" Bridgette asked roughly.

Bob looked over his shoulder at Amelia then back to Bridgette. He stared down at her breast swelling over the brassier cut of her dress. His phallus pounded tightly as it pushed against the fabric that, with little effect, concealed its identity.

"You are the maid aren't you?" Bob asked wisely.

"The disk," Bridgette said holding out her hand palm up. "you came to my apartment and took with you a disk. Where is it. I want it now." She demanded.

"Oh," Amelia said walking up to Bob's side. "her apartment huh."

Bob was confused. "What disk?"

Bridgette grabbed Bob by the throat and lifted him off his feet. The throbbing in his phallus weakened quickly as he clutched, with both hands around her wrist. Bridgette looked down at his jeans then back into Bob's eyes. With a slanted eyed frown that smacked insanity, she whispered.

"I'm gonna' make those boxers a pouch for shit." She said evenly.

Bob looked down and over at Amelia. His eyes almost pushing out over their lids. Sweat raced down the sides of his cheeks and his feet dangled, kicking minutely then stopping as her grip tightened.

"Amelia," Bob said in a dry croaking

whisper. "I think she means it."

Bridgette dropped Bob and he fell on his backside. He looked up at Bridgette with a simple angular expression.

"By the way," Bob said. "I loved you as the wicked witch in the Wizard of Oz."

Bridgette ignored him waving him off with a turn of her head.   "Amelia," Bridgette said politely. "Amelia Auer." She pronounced with clarity.

Bob watched as Amelia's legs gave out from under her. His mouth fell open and a responding denial followed by pitted flames exploded from his mouth setting Bridgette on fire. Amelia dropped dramatically to the floor.

"No, no, no," he repeated shaking his head.

Amelia lied on her side, eyes closed as if not to disturb demons, completely motionless.

He reached for her and pulled away. Bob stood. The power coming from somewhere as if he had to react soon. A mother's child pinned under a car, that power as he turned to see a ball of flame leap out the cavity in the Southeast wall. Again he turned to Amelia. With two steps he was kneeling at her side. Bob turned Amelia on her back and gentle lifted her head.

He bent to kiss her. He breathed in a sweet-sour smell, like that of a dying orchard. Her lips parted and Bob breathed into her mouth. Almost immediately, Amelia's face and hair caught fire. Bob pulled away; stunned. He began to pat her head softly then harder as it became impossible by this means to put the flames out. Her skin pealed and melted away. Her hair crackled and sizzled leaving her skull partly bald. Bob's hands caught fire and with several waves went out. He ran feverishly through the apartment and disappeared in the shadows. He returned with a broom and raised it high above his head. His arms shook nervously. It was the thought of hurting her, not knowing if she were dead or barely alive. He dropped the broom and ran out into the shadows again. He appeared, his body soaked and his eyes bright and smeary. He jumped over a particle piece of David expertly leveling the water inside the ceramic cup. A cup he gave her just for the thought of giving, no special reason or occasion, just a cup.

In red bold letters it read: 'I love you.' He tripped over something his senses didn't realize was there. He fought for balance hopping on one foot but fell, controlling his fall with one arm stretched out. The cup slipped from his hand. He scooted across glass and broken pieces that once formed great works of art. The cup bounced once and the water splashed out. It bobbled twice then broke.

Bob watched as the water rippled across the floor. His breathing was thick to an absolute hyper-ventilating black-out as the water stopped inches away from Amelia's smoking skull and seeped into a thin crevice in the wood flooring.

He covered himself in his arms and cried softly until it became out right balling.

On the other side of her head, unnoticed by Bob, the compact spun on its side like a spinning top. It wobbled, then stopped.

Her vanity, captured. Stored in its reflection the beauty that follows death, for whatever reason can happen at any time, any minute, anywhere.

One year later

She had designed new programs for computers. She also made friends with the access codes by creating a simple code that randomly questioned their central-computer millions of times per second using updated computations and combinations. It was an act that in time tapped into most computers security. Her lap-top had already typed out the passwords. She started to type. A moment later she was hooked up to a major companies computer. It was simple enough. Wire transfer billions of dollars to various accounts all over the world and scrap a little off in cash and move on. She put the phone onto the modems cradle, closed the lap-top and stood.

As she stood there, quietly surveying the small room, consulting every detail to memory he heard him say to her. "The best commodity one could have is information."

She picked up the lap-top and wiped a speckle of dust off the rosewood desk. Other than the computer, telephone, printer, paper shredder, desk, and chair, the room was completely empty of living convinces.

She sighed, satisfied, and left.

***

Autumn permeated the night air and crinkled leaves to scrape across the dark sidewalk. Her mink suede shoes made no sound as she walked hurriedly to her appointment. She was already late and he was so sweet and never hassled her about her tardiness.

The wind whistled through the young maple to her left and she quickened her pace if that was at all possible. She was already at an even trot and not once did she consider taking a cab. Cab drivers take records of their comings and goings. She worried little about who saw her on the dark streets. There must be millions of women who fit my description she would say if questioned. But to practice an alibi at this stage, as if she needed one was observed. She made a left on Columbus and crossed the street.

There was one other thing on her mind as she skipped up onto the curb. Revenge. She'd kill him tonight and that was that.

***

Bob walked lazily along Lake Michigan with petty worries swimming in his mind. She had come to him, every night, in his dreams. She just stood there, looking as if waiting for him to speak. He tried taking her to the moon and just when it would appear they'd reach it, the dream retracted and there she stood.

From the corner of his eye he caught a splash of bright orange. It flickered from the brightness of the street lamps giving an appearance as if someone's house was on fire. He almost passed it in his dream-like daze and decided to walk in its direction.

It was a medium sized maple tree which blazed bright crimson on its lower branches, burned vivid yellows and oranges in its center, and simmered deep burgundy at its top like the messy whirl of an artist's palette. The lamps shined brightly on the fiery colors that cascaded thin rivulets of pale-green leaves and blotches of deep-green leaves that hadn't been touched by autumn. It was a beautiful wonder as Bob stepped closer, hands buried deep inside his pockets.

From his distance he noticed that there

were no leaves on the top branches as the leaves that shed lay like a scarlet carpet around its trunk. Bob was caught up in the pivot of the pastiche that sounded inside his head.

He continued to walk mindlessly looking skyward piecing together thoughts, dreams, and music. Bob walked into a low tree branch which caught him under his chin jerking his head back. He fell to the Earth with a hollowed thud. He glanced upward, and the canopy of the tree parted ever so slightly, allowing him a fog-shrouded glimpse of a full moon. He squeezed his eyes together. His dream did not lack clarity and he drifted.

Bob stalked her for five hours, waiting for her to make her move. It had been days since he had-had a good long drink of life and he wouldn't go another day without it. He couldn't. It was either this or die.

Animals gave to much fight and offered little blood. Since Amelia had left him he studied change but it was a ritual to stalk the not-very-elusive.

She made a left through the park-and-lock on Van Buren and Dearborn Street and stood inside waiting on the elevator.

He watched her come out of Lawry's on east Ontario and walk in and out of five different office buildings. Her skirt snapped behind her as if she hadn't a worry in the world. She didn't hail a cab and never talked to anyone that he noticed. He wanted the darkness and the hours to deepen. Bob felt that queer sensation of surprise was evenly possible during the hours of darkness for which rest and sleep came so naturally for humans.

There were other preys that night but Bob wanted this one. She dressed conservatively with an expensive burgundy skirt suit, pumps, and black stockings. Her hair bounced with springing curls over her shoulder like an expensive wig. Like many women he saw that night there was really nothing special about this one except the way her breast laid over the square cut of her blouse. Her nipples piercing points could be seen a block away. It had slut written all over it and Bob liked sluts.

He stepped up behind her and she turned on him. She had enormous blue eyes, the eyes the mentally superior sometimes do that seemed to reflect more light than was available to them. Her skin was tan with no make-up except for a hint of mascara around the eyes.

Bob blinked trying to regain his composure. He felt weak and she grabbed his hand almost too tightly he thought as the sweet scent of her perfume paraded around his face. What happened next and the ten months that followed was always a blur to him.

Spring was heavy with the raging hormones of romance as they walked hand in hand along Lake Michigan. Almost grotesquely, their gray-black shadows exaggerated their size.

She took him home and amazingly, Bob went. She slipped off her jacket. Her silk blouse seemed glued across her strong breast. She stepped out of her shoes and walked towards Bob. She leaned over and whispered in Bob's ear, grabbed his hand and pulled him off the stool. He needed a drink. The draining weakness was taking over him, but he followed her.

They stepped into a room and instantly it was flooded with light. She unbuttoned her blouse and her large breast leaped out at him. Her nipples were dark lavender against the lighter tan of her breast. The crystal-blue eyes were an odd touch for a black woman but he followed the heat in his loins that said take her, or was it Candy as he looked down at his swollen phallus. His dick hadn't shriveled up at all he thought. He'd have his way with her first and then drink her blood.

He felt weak again and steadied himself against the jab of the door. She stepped into the shower and waved him in. Bob stepped over the ceramic basin and she cut the shower on. Beads of water rolled down the valley of her chest.

She raised up her skirt. She wore no

panties and quickly, by the shoulders gently pushed Bob to sit in the tub. The rest was welcomed as she bent over him and released his burning phallus. She held him roughly, sitting on her hunches. Bob weakened to almost passing out as he gasped for breath. She began writhing, inviting him in, her breast pressed against his face. His head began to spin like a propeller as he slipped.

"You're as clumsy as a one legged man in an ass kicking contest." She said.

"What?"

Bob opened his eyes and rubbed them as in the dream no one talked like that. He looked up into the varied nations of colors of the leaves as they rustled to unseen winds.

"What didn't you understand?" The voice high above him said.

The face was oblong but fairly recognizable. He was still dreaming and laughed slightly.

Bob jumped up and grabbed her. He squeezed her tightly then kissed her on her cheek.

"I love you." Bob said wholesomely.

"I love you more." Amelia challenged.

He kissed her again full on the lips and stepped back.

"I've missed you."

She simply smiled and grabbed his hand. "Yeah, right."

Bob placed an arm over Amelia's shoulder. They disappeared beyond the stone Buckingham Fountain.

"Is this the part where I get to slap you

around?" Bob questioned.

"Yeah, right."

***

She walked up to the maple tree and looked around. He was late or she was early and looked down at her watch. He had nothing else to do she thought and stomped her foot.

"Where is he?"

The wind blew from off the lake brushing her hair aside. A scar on the left side of her neck became visible. Her visual tracking conducted a typical saccadic sweep. Her eyes now bright yellow rose defiantly toward the black, starlit sky as the acting sentinel of

Chicago, the Willis Tower was now their first of many future attempts to reach the moon.

No one could stop the laughter, or hear it.

THE END

kewodignet.com

www.ingramcontent.com/pod-product-compliance
Lightning Source LLC
Chambersburg PA
CBHW060803030726
47503CB00002B/316